ALIENS
vs.
PREDATOR

Randy Stradley
script

Phill Norwood
pencils, pages 7-126; pencils and inks, pages 161-168

Chris Warner
pencils, pages 129-158

Karl Story
inks, pages 7-96

Robert Campanella
inks, pages 99-158

Pat Brosseau
letters

In-Color
colors

Randy Stradley and Diana Schutz
series editors

Jerry Prosser and Randy Stradley
collection editors

Phill Norwood
cover and spot illustrations

*This material originally appeared in Dark Horse Presents #34-36,
Aliens Vs. Predator #1-4, and Dark Horse Presents Fifth Anniversary Special*

TABLE OF CONTENTS

Mike Richardson • publisher
Neil Hankerson • vice-president of operations
Randy Stradley • executive editor
Barbara Kesel • managing editor
Bob Schreck • marketing director
Brad Horn • controller
Cece Cutsforth • production director
Chris Chalenor • production manager
Sean Tierney • DTP manager
Anina Bennett, Jerry Prosser, Diana Schutz,
and Chris Warner • editorial staff
Steven Birch, Cary Grazzini, Ray Gruen,
Carolyn Megyesi, Greg Pearson, Jack Pollock, Steve Posey,
and Monty Sheldon • production
Kris Young • marketing assistant
Debbie Byrd, Chris Creviston, Tiffany Schlobohm • operations

ALIENS VS. PREDATOR
ISBN # 1-878574-27-2
Published by Dark Horse Comics, Inc.
10956 S.E. Main St., Milwaukie, OR 97222
USA

Second Printing
2 4 6 8 10 9 7 5 3

Story and art copyright © 1989, 1990, and 1991
Twentieth Century Fox Film Corporation
Afterword text and art copyright © 1991 Randy Stradley Phill Norwood

chapter

1

"THE CRACKS IN OUR TECHNOLOGY"

Sometime in the future...

commercial transport vessel 'The Lector'
crew: fifteen
cargo: rendering plant processing
        15,000,000 tons of fish and
        animal products
course: ranching outpost Prosperity Wells,
        on the planet Ryushi

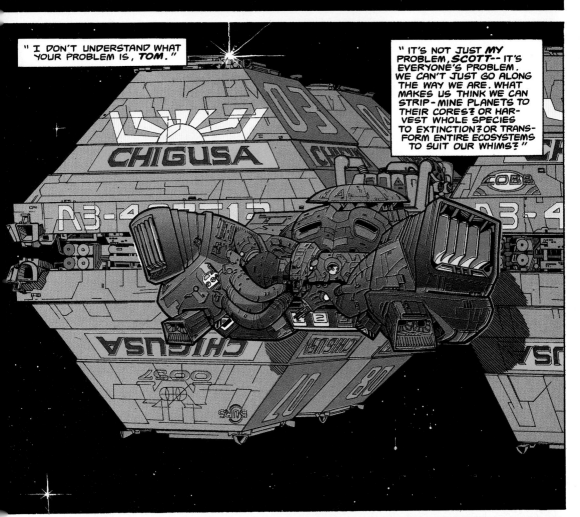

"I DON'T UNDERSTAND WHAT YOUR PROBLEM IS, *TOM.*"

"IT'S NOT JUST *MY* PROBLEM, *SCOTT* -- IT'S EVERYONE'S PROBLEM. WE CAN'T JUST GO ALONG THE WAY WE ARE. WHAT MAKES US THINK WE CAN STRIP-MINE PLANETS TO THEIR CORES? OR HARVEST WHOLE SPECIES TO EXTINCTION? OR TRANSFORM ENTIRE ECOSYSTEMS TO SUIT OUR WHIMS?"

I KNOW I'M UGLY BUT MY MAMA LOVES ME

BE REALISTIC, TOM -- EVERYONE KNEW EARTH'S RESOURCES WOULDN'T LAST FOREVER. WHAT ARE WE SUPPOSED TO DO, IGNORE THE OTHER RESOURCES AVAILABLE TO US BECAUSE A MILLION YEARS FROM NOW THEY *MIGHT* BE OF SOME USE TO AN EMERGING LIFE FORM?

WHOA--!

THAT WAS CLOSE!

"WE'RE REGISTERING A POWER SURGE! WHAT THE HELL WAS THAT THING?"

"THE SCANNERS SAY IT'S MOSTLY METALLIC-- BUT WHATEVER IT IS, IT'S MOVING WAY TOO FAST TO BE ANYTHING MANMADE."

"YEAH, IT'S PROBABLY JUST A METEOR. ANYHOW, AS I WAS SAYING, DO WE JUST TELL EVERYONE, 'HEY, SHOW'S OVER. EVERYTHING WE NEED IS ON THIS OTHER PLANET OVER HERE--'

"--BUT WE CAN'T USE ANY OF IT BECAUSE IT RIGHTFULLY BELONGS TO THE SINGLE-CELL ORGANISMS THAT LIVE THERE'?"

"YOU'RE TAKING THIS ARGUMENT TO A RIDICULOUS EXTREME, SCOTT."

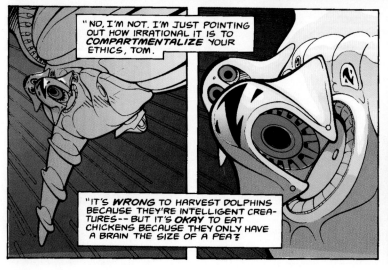

"NO, I'M NOT. I'M JUST POINTING OUT HOW IRRATIONAL IT IS TO COMPARTMENTALIZE YOUR ETHICS, TOM.

"IT'S WRONG TO HARVEST DOLPHINS BECAUSE THEY'RE INTELLIGENT CREATURES-- BUT IT'S OKAY TO EAT CHICKENS BECAUSE THEY ONLY HAVE A BRAIN THE SIZE OF A PEA?

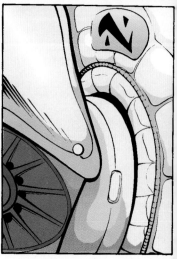

"ULTIMATELY, EVERY DISTINCTION IS *SUBJECTIVE,* AND ANY LINE YOU DRAW IS *ARTIFICIAL.*

"WHO'S TO SAY WHAT *POTENTIAL* LIES WITHIN A CHICKEN-- OR EVEN ITS *EGG?*"

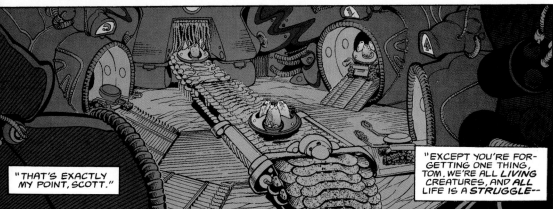

"THAT'S EXACTLY MY POINT, SCOTT."

"EXCEPT YOU'RE FORGETTING ONE THING, TOM. WE'RE ALL *LIVING* CREATURES, AND *ALL* LIFE IS A *STRUGGLE--*

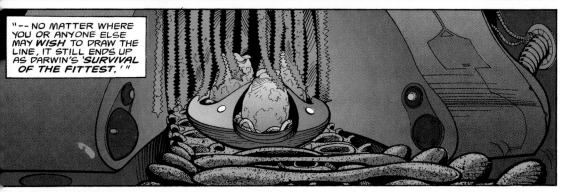

"-- NO MATTER WHERE YOU OR ANYONE ELSE MAY *WISH* TO DRAW THE LINE, IT STILL ENDS UP AS DARWIN'S *'SURVIVAL OF THE FITTEST.'*"

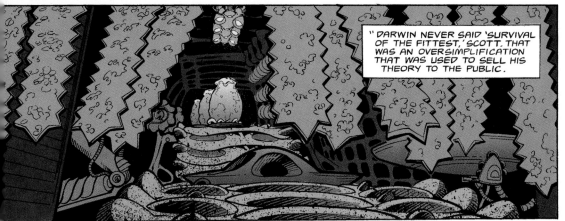

"DARWIN NEVER SAID 'SURVIVAL OF THE FITTEST,' SCOTT. THAT WAS AN OVERSIMPLIFICATION THAT WAS USED TO SELL HIS THEORY TO THE PUBLIC."

"WHAT YOU'RE TALKING ABOUT IS *MANIFEST DESTINY*."

"YOU CAN CALL IT WHATEVER YOU WANT, TOM.

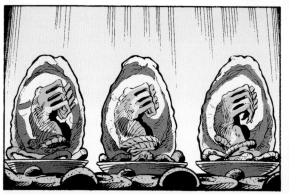

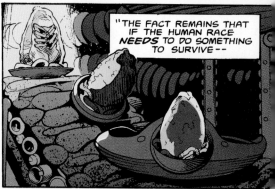

"THE FACT REMAINS THAT IF THE HUMAN RACE *NEEDS* TO DO SOMETHING TO SURVIVE--

"--AND THE LOWER ORDERS DON'T HAVE THE POWER TO *STOP* US--

"--WE'LL PREVAIL.

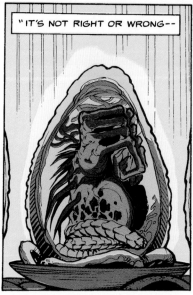

"IT'S NOT RIGHT OR WRONG--

"--IT'S JUST THE WAY THINGS ARE.

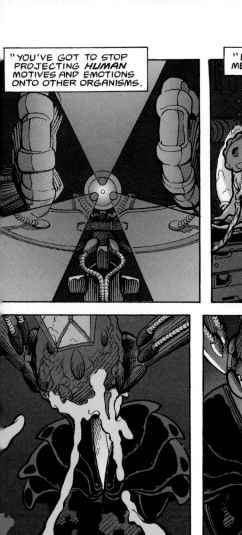

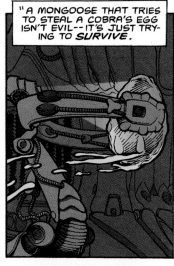

"YOU'VE GOT TO STOP PROJECTING *HUMAN* MOTIVES AND EMOTIONS ONTO OTHER ORGANISMS.

"EVERYTHING IS MERELY WHAT IT IS.

"A MONGOOSE THAT TRIES TO STEAL A COBRA'S EGG ISN'T EVIL-- IT'S JUST TRYING TO *SURVIVE*.

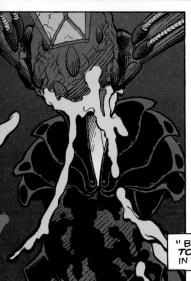

"BUT THE COBRA IS TRYING TO SURVIVE, *TOO*. AND IF IT CATCHES THE MONGOOSE IN ITS NEST, THERE'S GOING TO BE A FIGHT.

"FORTUNATELY FOR THE MONGOOSE, IT HAS *FASTER* REFLEXES AND A MORE *EFFICIENT* METABOLISM.

"WHETHER THAT'S *'FAIR'* OR NOT ISN'T EVEN PART OF THE EQUATION-- IT'S SIMPLY THE *WAY THINGS ARE*."

"YEAH? TRY TELLING THAT TO THE COBRA.

"BUT FOR THE SAKE OF ARGUMENT, WE'LL *IGNORE* THE QUESTION OF ETHICS. STILL, ALL YOU'RE SAYING, SCOTT, IS THAT IT'S ALL RIGHT TO DO *WHATEVER* WE WANT--

"--TO EXPLOIT ANY ECOSYSTEM, ANY SPECIES--

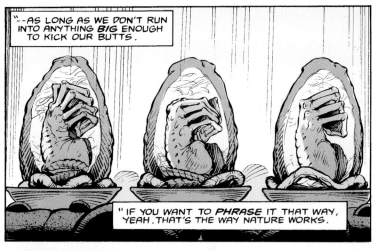

"--AS LONG AS WE DON'T RUN INTO ANYTHING *BIG* ENOUGH TO KICK OUR BUTTS.

"IF YOU WANT TO *PHRASE* IT THAT WAY, YEAH. THAT'S THE WAY NATURE WORKS.

"SURE, ON TUTORING DISKS--

"--BUT NOT IN THE *REAL* WORLD. EVERY PART OF AN ECOSYSTEM IS *DEPENDENT* ON EVERY OTHER PART.

"IT'S THAT INTERDEPEN-DENCY THAT MAKES INTERFERING WITH EXISTING SYSTEMS SO CHANCY.

"EVEN THE SMALLEST COMPONENTS ARE *VITALLY* IMPORTANT.

"WHO WOULD HAVE GUESSED THAT MILLIONS OF 'KILLER BEES' COULD SPRING FROM A *HANDFUL* OF ESCAPED AFRICAN BEES?"

"OR THAT A FEW BRAZILIAN FIRE ANTS COULD MAKE THE SOUTHEASTERN PORTION OF THE U.S. VIRTUALLY *UNINHABITABLE* IN JUST OVER SEVENTY YEARS?"

"AND WHAT ABOUT THE 'OIL-EATING' BACTERIUM THE GENE-SPLICERS AT THE PETROLEUM COMPANIES DEVELOPED TO CLEAN UP THEIR SPILLS?"

"REMEMBER HOW THEY THOUGHT THEY HAD IT *COMPLETELY* IN THEIR CONTROL?"

"COME ON, TOM, THE OIL WOULD'VE *DRIED UP* SOONER OR LATER ANYWAY, AND I HEAR THE NEW *REPRO-INHIBITORS* THEY'RE USING ARE MAKING A SUBSTANTIAL DENT IN THE FIRE ANT POPULATIONS--"

"--SURE, WE SUFFER SETBACKS, BUT WE'LL *ALWAYS* FIND WAYS *AROUND* THE PROBLEMS THAT NATURE THROWS AT US."

"WILL WE, SCOTT?"

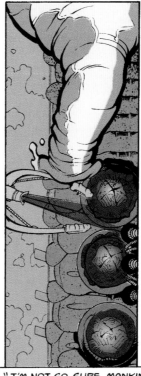

"I'M NOT SO SURE. MANKIND NEVER SEEMS TO LEARN. WE GET OUR HANDS SLAPPED ON A REGULAR BASIS, BUT WE STILL CAN'T SEEM TO KEEP THEM TO OURSELVES.

"THE TIGHTER THE GRIP WE TRY TO GET ON NATURE, THE MORE NATURE PUSHES THROUGH THE CRACKS IN OUR TECHNOLOGY.

"AND WITH SOME OF THE THINGS WE'RE ENCOUNTERING IN THE SETTLEMENTS, WE HAVE NO IDEA OF WHAT KIND OF TROUBLE WE MAY BE LETTING OURSELVES IN FOR BY MESSING AROUND."

"WELL, SO FAR WE'VE DONE OKAY:

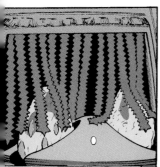

ON ALL OF THE LIFE-SUPPORTING PLANETS WE'VE COME ACROSS, THE WORST THING WE'VE EVER ENCOUNTERED HAS BEEN THE 'BLOOD WILLIES' OF EPSILON INDI TWO.

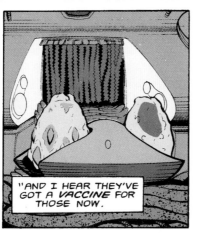

"AND I HEAR THEY'VE GOT A VACCINE FOR THOSE NOW.

"IF I WERE YOU, I'D PUT MY FAITH IN SCIENCE AND STOP WORRYING ABOUT THE BOGEY MAN. AND I'D WATCH WHAT I SAID AROUND THE CORPORATE TYPES, TOM--"

"--ALL ANY OF THEM CARE ABOUT IS THEIR JOBS, AND YOU'LL MAKE THEM *NERVOUS* WITH TALK ABOUT PROBLEMS THAT DON'T EXIST YET."

"I DON'T CARE. THIS IS MY *LAST* LONG HAUL. I'M GETTING OUT WHILE THE GETTING'S GOOD.

"ALL OF THE MONKEYING AROUND THE CORPORATIONS ARE DOING OUT IN THE SETTLEMENTS MAY NOT BOTHER *YOU*, SCOTT, BUT IT DOES ME.

"WE'VE HAD A LONG RUN OF GOOD FORTUNE--LONGER THAN WE'VE DESERVED. THERE'S A MAJOR LEAGUE *TURD* COMING DOWN THE PIKE, MARK MY WORDS--

"--AND *I* DON'T WANT TO BE AROUND WHEN IT HITS THE FAN.

" I'M TELLING YOU WE SHOULDN'T BE MESSING WITH *MOTHER NATURE*:

"SHE'S A REAL *BITCH.*

chapter

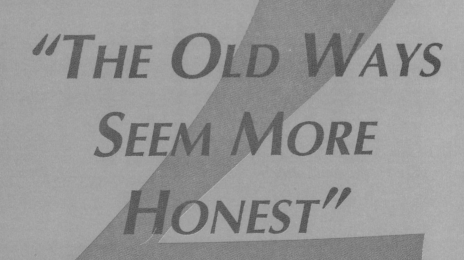

2

"The Old Ways Seem More Honest"

'WE HAVE TO LEARN TO WORK *WITH* NATURE. THIS *RELIANCE* ON TECHNOLOGY IS GETTING TO BE TOO MUCH FOR ME, SCOTT.

" IT'S NO LONGER A MEANS TO AN END-- IT'S BECOME AN *END* UNTO ITSELF. WE USE IT LIKE A WALL BETWEEN OURSELVES AND OUR SURROUNDINGS...

KLICK

" BETWEEN OURSELVES--

"--AND WHO WE *REALLY* ARE.

"WE'VE COME A LONG WAY IN THE PAST THREE THOUSAND YEARS--

"--BUT I CAN'T HELP FEELING THAT WE'VE *LOST* AS MUCH AS WE'VE GAINED."

"SO WHAT'S YOUR *SOLUTION*, TOM? GIVE UP MODERN CONVENIENCES AND GO BACK TO STONE KNIVES AND SQUATTING IN CAVES?

"YOU'RE REACHING FOR EXTREMES AGAIN, SCOTT, BUT--

CLICK

CLICK

SNAP

"-- THAT JUST *MIGHT* BE WHAT IT TAKES TO PUT US BACK ON THE RIGHT TRACK.

"I'M TALKING ABOUT THE *CHALLENGE* OF PUTTING AWAY THE *CRUTCHES* OF OUR TECHNOLOGY--

"AND I'M NOT TALKING ABOUT *AUSTERITY* OR *DEPRIVATION*.

"-- AND GOING BACK TO RELYING ON OUR OWN *STRENGTH* AND *CUNNING*.

THESE DAYS WE'RE SO INSULATED THAT WE [MA]KE HEROES OUT OF *ANYONE* WHO DARES TO FACE UP TO A CHALLENGE.

"BUT IT WASN'T ALWAYS LIKE THAT. LIFE OR DEATH CHALLENGES USED TO BE AN EVERY-DAY THING--

"--AND *REAL* MEN DIDN'T *WAIT* FOR ADVENTURE TO COME TO THEM. THEY RUSHED OUT TO MEET IT--

"--NOT LIKE THE *GENERALS* AND *CORPORATE HEADS* THESE DAYS WHO SEND OUT THE *LITTLE GUYS* TO DO THEIR DIRTY WORK.

SLAP

IT USED TO BE THAT A MAN'S [S]TANDING AS A LEADER WAS [DE]TERMINED BY HOW HE [HANDLED HIMSELF--

[--IN THE FACE] OF DANGER."

21

"YEAH, YEAH-- VERY NOSTALGIC, TOM, VERY *MACHO*. BUT IT'S NOT VERY PRACTICAL IN THIS DAY AND AGE. CAN YOU SEE A BUNCH OF CORPORATE VPs DUKING IT OUT FOR THE RIGHT TO BE *CEO*?"

"OR MAYBE *YOU* AND *ME* GOING AT EACH OTHER WITH KNIVES TO SEE WHO GETS A BETTER PILOT'S RATING?"

"HEY, EVERY CULTURE OBSERVES ITS OWN RITUALS FOR ESTABLISHING STATUS. LOOK AT THE INFIGHTING AND BACK-STABBING THAT GOES ON AT EVERY LEVEL OF *OUR* SOCIETY.

"AND WE'RE STILL FIGHTING OVER THE *SAME THINGS*--

"--PROPERTY, LEADERSHIP--

"-- TERRITORIAL RIGHTS.

"THE ONLY DIFFERENCE IS OUR METHODS HAVE BECOME MORE SUBTLE, LESS DIRECT.

"SOMEHOW THE OLD WAYS SEEM MORE *HONEST.* "

"THEN YOU'VE GOT THE NEIGHBORHOOD BULLY CALLING THE SHOTS-- YOU'RE BACK TO *PACK* MENTALITY."

"YOU'RE AN IDEALIST, TOM. WHAT HAPPENS WHEN THE *WRONG GUY* WINS?"

"THERE ARE CHECKS AND BALANCES IN EVERY SYSTEM, SCOTT."

"YEAH, BUT YOUR WAY LEAVES THEM ALL UP TO *INDIVIDUAL* INITIATIVE!

"WITHOUT SOME KIND OF SANCTIONED AVENUE FOR DISSENT--

"--A GUY WOULD HAVE TO BE A REAL HERO--

"--OR A REAL *FOOL* TO BUTT HEADS WITH THE CHIEF."

K-RACK

"SO? ARE THINGS REALLY SO DIFFERENT FOR *US*? YOU'RE THE ONE THAT'S ALWAYS TELLING ME TO WATCH WHAT I SAY AROUND THE DESK JOCKEYS--

"--WHERE'S *MY* 'SANCTIONED AVENUE FOR DISSENT'?

RRRRRRREAR

"AT LEAST IF I BUST A GUY IN THE CHOPS, HE CLEARLY UNDERSTANDS THAT I DON'T LIKE WHAT HE'S DOING."

"THERE YOU GO WITH YOUR *IDEALISM* AGAIN. YOU'RE TRYING TO ROMANTICIZE THIS INTO TWO TIGERS BRAWLING TO DETERMINE DOMINANCE—— OR RIGHTS TO A FAVORITE HUNTING AREA.

" IN THE SAME SITUATION HUMANS WOULD JUST *KILL* EACH OTHER. WE'VE '*OUT-GROWN*' THE INSTINCT FOR *SPECIES PRESERVATION* THAT PREVENTS THAT IN THE LOWER ORDERS--

"-- BUT WE HAVEN'T TRULY GROWN *INTO* THE MORALITY THAT YOU'RE SO FOND OF CITING, TOM.

" THE SOCIETY WE'VE BUILT ISN'T PERFECT, GRANTED. BUT IT *WORKS*--PROBABLY MORE *BECAUSE* OF OUR LEVEL OF TECHNOLOGY THAN IN SPITE OF IT.

" HOW MANY GUYS WOULDN'T WANT TO TRADE THEIR BORING, EARTHSIDE JOB FOR *YOURS*-- A JOB MADE POSS-IBLE BY *TECHNOLOGY?*

" BUT IF YOU WANT TO GET BACK TO NATURE, THERE RE WAYS TO DO IT--

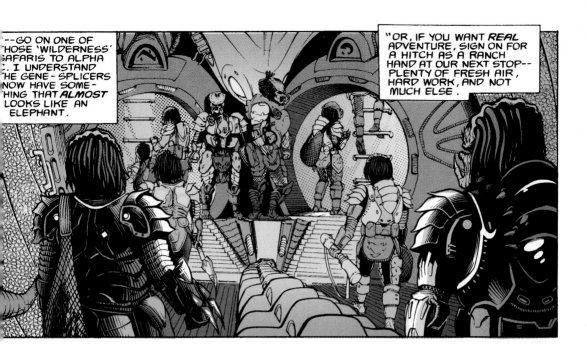

"--GO ON ONE OF THOSE 'WILDERNESS' SAFARIS TO ALPHA C. I UNDERSTAND THE GENE-SPLICERS NOW HAVE SOMETHING THAT *ALMOST* LOOKS LIKE AN ELEPHANT.

"OR, IF YOU WANT *REAL* ADVENTURE, SIGN ON FOR A HITCH AS A RANCH HAND AT OUR NEXT STOP-- PLENTY OF FRESH AIR, HARD WORK, AND NOT MUCH ELSE.

"MAYBE THAT'S *YOUR* IDEA OF FULFILLMENT--

"--THOUGH I CAN'T IMAGINE ANYONE ENVYING YOU THE JOB.

"ME, I CAN GET ENOUGH ADVENTURE FROM THE VIDS. GOD BLESS MODERN TECHNOLOGY!

chapter

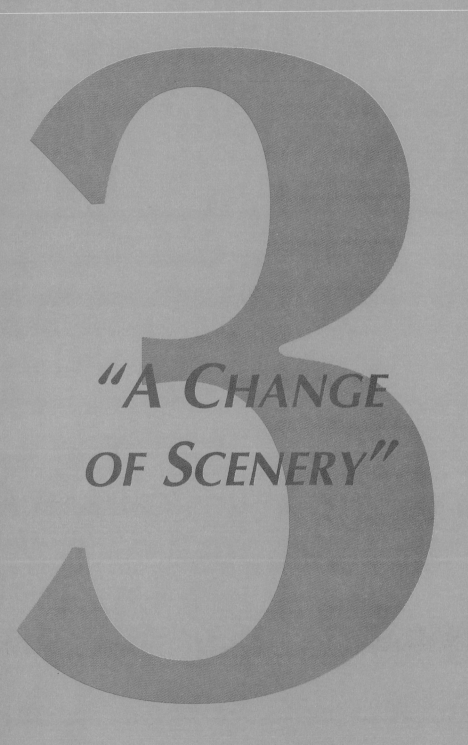

3

"A CHANGE OF SCENERY"

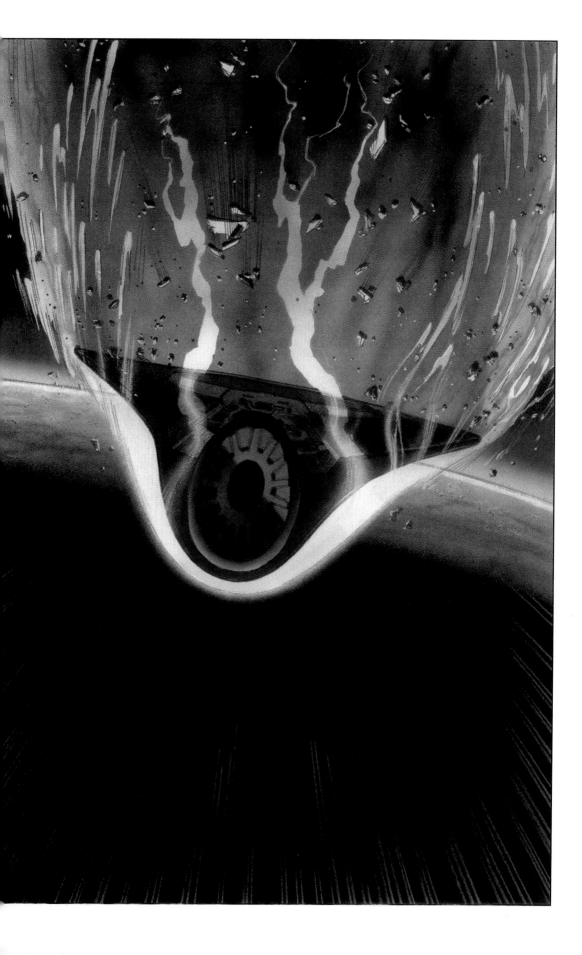

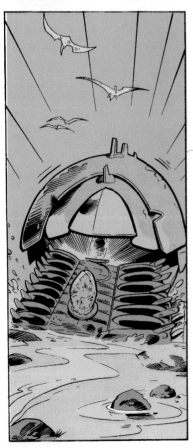

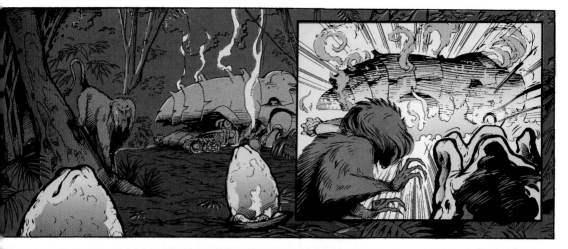

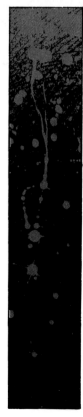

"YOU'RE BEING AWFULLY QUIET, TOM."

"WHAT'S THE MATTER-- YOU MAD AT ME?"

"HUH? UH, NO, SCOTT. I WAS JUST *THINKING*."

"LOOK, I KNOW YOU SAID IT AS A JOKE-- BUT MAYBE I *SHOULD* GO ON ONE OF THOSE SAFARIS--

"--OR SIGN ON AS A RANCH HAND."

34

"MAYBE IT'LL TURN OUT THAT YOU'RE RIGHT, AND I WOULDN'T LIKE IT. BUT I SHOULD AT LEAST GIVE IT A *TRY*.

"A CHANGE OF SCENERY MIGHT BE JUST WHAT I NEED...

"GET BACK TO THE LAND AND LIVING THINGS ...

GET SOME ADVENTURE AND UNCERTAINTY BACK INTO MY LIFE.

"DID I EVER TELL YOU THAT I WENT *HUNTING* ONCE ?"

"I HAD AN UNCLE WHO WAS WEALTHY. HE TOOK ME QUAIL HUNTING WHEN I TURNED FIFTEEN--SAID IT WOULD MAKE A *MAN* OF ME. BUT ALL I COULD THINK ABOUT WAS HOW *BIG* MY SHOTGUN WAS, AND HOW *SMALL* THE BIRDS WERE.

"I GUESS I COULD UNDERSTAND THE *POTENTIAL* FOR EXCITEMENT IN THE HUNT, BUT FOR ME THE THRILL WAS MISSING.

"THE CONTEST SEEMED SO LOPSIDED. I WONDERED WHAT IT WOULD BE LIKE TO HUNT SOMETHING THAT WAS CAPA-BLE OF HUNTING *ME*:

"THE CHALLENGE--

"-- THE DANGER.

"TO PUT YOURSELF ON AN *EQUAL FOOTING* WITH NATURE --

"...THAT'S GOT TO BE THE *ULTIMATE* THRILL!

"--TO RISK *EVERY-THING* ON YOUR OWN SKILL AND STRENGTH...

" I MEAN, LOOK AT WHAT WE *DO* FOR A LIVING-- ACCESS THE COMPUTER, PUNCH A FEW BUTTONS-- ALL THE WORK IS DONE *FOR* US. *ANYBODY* COULD DO THIS JOB, WITH THE RIGHT *TRAINING*.

" I WANT TO DO SOMETHING THAT'LL GET MY HEART POUNDING.

"I GUESS *THAT'S* WHAT I MEANT BY MY ANTI-TECHNOLOGY TIRADE. IT'S NOT THAT TECHNOLOGY IS EVIL IN AND OF *ITSELF*--

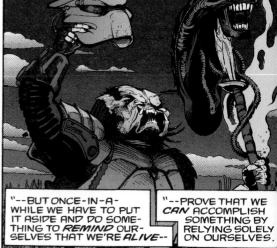

"--BUT ONCE-IN-A-WHILE WE HAVE TO PUT IT ASIDE AND DO SOME-THING TO *REMIND* OUR-SELVES THAT WE'RE *ALIVE*--

"--PROVE THAT WE *CAN* ACCOMPLISH SOMETHING BY RELYING SOLELY ON OURSELVES.

"I CAN'T HELP BUT THINK AN EXPERIENCE LIKE THAT WOULD *CHANGE* A PERSON--

"-- MAYBE NOT IN A WAY THAT *OTHER* PEOPLE WOULD NOTICE --

"-- BUT IT WOULD BE SOMETHING YOU'D CARRY WITH YOU FOR THE REST OF YOUR LIFE.

"I KNOW WHAT YOU MEAN, TOM. KINDA LIKE THE FIRST TIME YOU GET LAID, RIGHT? DID I EVER TELL YOU ABOUT THAT? I WAS AT THIS PARTY, SEE, AND--"

"OH, BROTHER..."

chapter

4

"SOMEBODY'S IDEA OF PARADISE"

The planet Ryushi, at the edge of the
Chigusa Corporation's holdings in the
Beta Cygni system

only human outpost: Prosperity Wells
population: 113, primarily freelance
ranchers and their
families, plus a token staff
of corporate overseers

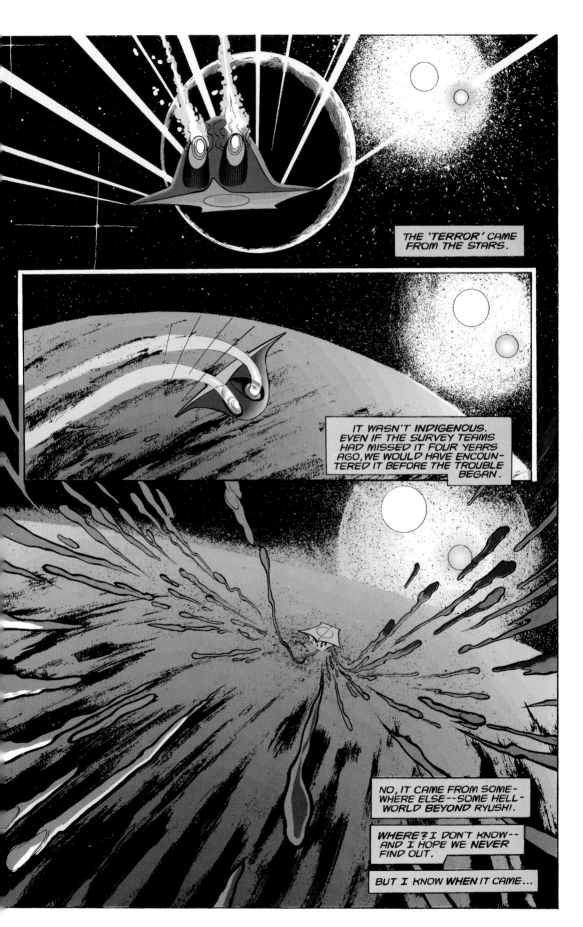

THE 'TERROR' CAME
FROM THE STARS.

IT WASN'T INDIGENOUS.
EVEN IF THE SURVEY TEAMS
HAD MISSED IT FOUR YEARS
AGO, WE WOULD HAVE ENCOUN-
TERED IT BEFORE THE TROUBLE
BEGAN.

NO, IT CAME FROM SOME-
WHERE ELSE--SOME HELL-
WORLD BEYOND RYUSHI.

WHERE? I DON'T KNOW--
AND I HOPE WE NEVER
FIND OUT.

BUT I KNOW WHEN IT CAME...

THE 'TERROR' ARRIVED AT HIGH NOON.

IN THE SEARING HEAT OF RYUSHI'S NINETEEN-HOUR DAYLIGHT PERIOD, NOTHING STIRS OF ITS OWN VOLITION-- NOT EVEN THE ARMORED FIRE CRAWLERS.

WITH EVERY LIVING CREATURE BURROWED IN, AESTIVATING, OR OTHERWISE SHELTERED AGAINST THE HEAT, IT'S NOT SURPRISING THERE WERE NO WITNESSES TO ITS ARRIVAL.

I'M GETTING SOMETHING ON THE LONG-RANGE SCANNERS--

CREAK
CREAK
CREAK

--IT'S COMING IN FAST AND SHALLOW. *MIGHT* BE A METEOR, BUT IT'S NOT SHOWING ANY SIGNS OF BREAKING UP.

BETTER ALERT THE BOSS.

RIGHT. *MR. SHIMURA*, WE HAVE AN UNIDENTIFIED AT--

OH, *MS. NOGUCHI*. I, UH, I HAVE A MESSAGE FOR MR. SHIMURA, IS HE THERE?

YES, HE'S HERE, BUT YOU CAN GIVE *ME* THE MESSAGE, MASON.

UH, YES, MA'AM. LONG RANGE IS SHOWING AN *UNIDENTIFIED*. IT'S PROBABLY JUST A METEOR, BUT IT LOOKS AS THOUGH IT MAY HIT--

BUT IF IT STAYS ON ITS PRESENT COURSE--

--IT'LL MAKE PLANET-FALL ABOUT THIRTY KLIKS NORTH OF HERE-- OPEN PASTURE.

OPEN PASTURE? THEN DON'T WORRY ABOUT IT. WE CAN INVESTIGATE *AFTER* THE ROUNDUP. NOGUCHI OUT.

WHAT'S IT TAKE, HIROKI? I'VE BEEN HERE NEARLY SIX MONTHS--BUT THEY'RE STILL REPORTING TO *YOU*.

THE RANCHERS, AND EVEN THE *STAFF* STILL TREAT ME LIKE I'M A STRANGER! I'VE DONE EVERYTHING I CAN THINK OF TO PUT MY STAMP ON THINGS AROUND HERE--TO MAKE THIS JOB *MINE!*

MAYBE *THAT'S* YOUR PROBLEM, MACHIKO.

YOU'RE TRYING TO ADAPT THE JOB TO *YOU*, RATHER THAN ADAPTING YOURSELF TO *IT*.

THIS IS A VERY NICE OFFICE YOU'VE BUILT FOR YOUR-SELF, BUT YOU CAN'T *RUN* AN OPERATION LIKE THIS AND *HIDE* FROM IT AT THE SAME TIME.

WHAT ARE YOU TRYING TO SAY, HIROKI?

LOOK, I'LL BE AROUND FOR ANOTHER WEEK OR SO--AFTER THAT YOU'RE ON YOUR *OWN*. IN THE MEAN-TIME, I'LL DO WHAT-EVER I CAN TO HELP YOU.

HIROKI...

DON'T FORGET THAT THESE ARE *HUMAN BEINGS* YOU'RE DEALING WIT[H] *TREAT* THEM AS SU[CH] AND IT WOULDN'T HURT FOR YOU TO LOOSEN UP SOME[-] EITHER.

GET OUT OF YOUR OFFICE ONCE IN AWH[ILE] GET YOUR HANDS DIR[TY] GET SOME *RHYNTH* *SHIT* BETWEEN YOUR TOES.

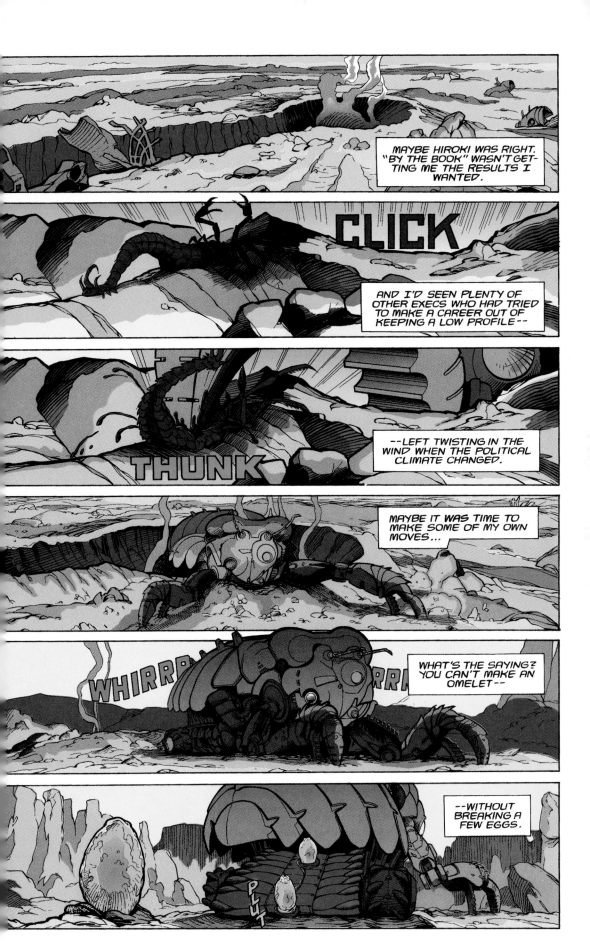

BUT YOUR ASSOCIATION HAS ALREADY *SIGNED* AN AGREEMENT WITH THE COMPANY, *ACKLAND!*

YEAH, BUT THAT WAS *BEFORE* WE SAW WHAT THE MARKET WAS DOING BACK ON EARTH. IF WE'D KNOWN THE PRICE OF MEAT WAS GOING TO JUMP LIKE THIS, WE'D HAVE ASKED FOR *MORE!*

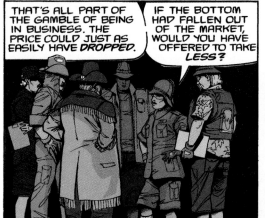

THAT'S ALL PART OF THE GAMBLE OF BEING IN BUSINESS. THE PRICE COULD JUST AS EASILY HAVE *DROPPED.*

IF THE BOTTOM HAD FALLEN OUT OF THE MARKET, WOULD YOU HAVE OFFERED TO TAKE *LESS?*

THAT'S NOT THE POINT, *HIROKI!* THE COMPANY'S MAKING A *KILLING* FROM OUR SWEAT AND WE'RE GETTING *SCREWED*-- RIGHT, ACKLAND?

THAT'S THE WAY THE *RANCHERS ASSOCIATION* SEES IT.

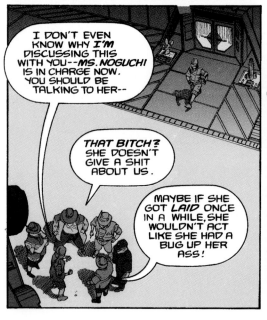

I DON'T EVEN KNOW WHY *I'M* DISCUSSING THIS WITH YOU--*MS. NOGUCHI* IS IN CHARGE NOW. YOU SHOULD BE TALKING TO HER--

THAT BITCH? SHE DOESN'T GIVE A SHIT ABOUT US.

MAYBE IF SHE GOT *LAID* ONCE IN A WHILE, SHE WOULDN'T ACT LIKE SHE HAD A BUG UP HER ASS!

I'D TAKE A PIECE OF *THAT* ACTION--

YOU *KIDDIN'?* PROBABLY FREEZE YOUR DICK OFF-- Uhh...

I THOUGHT WE WERE IN THE MIDDLE OF A *ROUNDUP*, GENTLEMEN!

COUGH COUGH

ACKLAND, I'LL *TALK* TO THE COMPANY AND SEE IF I CAN SWING A LARGER CUT FOR YOUR RANCHERS-- BUT THERE WON'T BE *ANYTHING* FOR *ANYONE* IF YOUR RHYNTH AREN'T READY FOR SHIPMENT BY THE TIME *THE LECTOR* ARRIVES.

REMEMBER-- STAGGERED SLEEP-ING SCHEDULES. THIS IS A *THIRTY-THREE* HOUR-A-DAY JOB!

"NOW, EVERYBODY *BACK TO WORK!* HIROKI-- READY TWO BIKES, WE'RE GOING OUT."

DON'T SAY IT. DON'T SAY *ANYTHING.*

THE RIDE THAT DAY WAS THE LONGEST I'D SPENT OUTDOORS SINCE ARRIVING ON RYUSHI. I'D ALWAYS THOUGHT OF THE PLANET AS NOTHING MORE THAN DESERT-- ONE SQUARE METER OF IT LOOKING JUST LIKE ANY OTHER SQUARE METER.

NOW, THANKS TO HIROKI, I WAS BEGINNING TO SEE RYUSHI IN A DIFFERENT LIGHT.

IT WAS STILL A HARSH, UNFORGIVING WORLD--

--WHERE ONE MISTAKE COULD LEAD TO DEATH-- BUT THERE WAS A BEAUTY AND DIVERSITY I HADN'T NOTICED BEFORE, AND THE TENUOUSNESS OF THAT BEAUTY MADE IT SOMEHOW MORE PRECIOUS.

I BEGAN TO UNDERSTAND THE RANCHERS-- WHAT IT WAS THAT MOVED THEM TO LEAVE EARTH AND MAKE RYUSHI THEIR HOME.

UNFORTUNATELY, IT WAS TOO LATE FOR THIS NEW UNDERSTANDING TO CHANGE MY STANDING WITH THE RANCHERS.

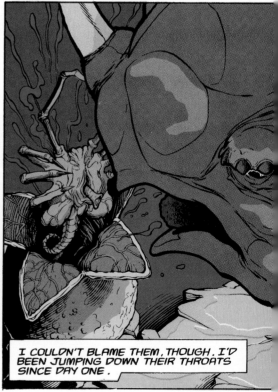

I COULDN'T BLAME THEM, THOUGH. I'D BEEN JUMPING DOWN THEIR THROATS SINCE DAY ONE.

ROTH, TAKE SOME OF THE BOYS AND RUN THESE THREE GULLIES. DRIVE 'EM DOWN INTO *BERIKI CANYON* AND HOOK UP WITH CHO'S GROUP.

WHAT'S THE *PROBLEM,* HIROKI? YOU AND THE BOSS-LADY GET LOST?

WE'RE JUST MAKING THE ROUNDS--

YEAH, RIGHT. SO WHAT'S THE *REAL* REASON FOR THE VISIT? THE COMPANY SHOOT DOWN THE PRICE INCREASE?

YOU KNOW *'LITTLE' CYGNI* PUTS OUT TOO MUCH MAGNETIC INTERFERENCE DURING THE *DAY* FOR US TO PATCH THROUGH TO EARTH. I'LL *CONTACT* THEM THIS EVENING.

AND I'LL DO ALL I CAN TO GET YOU A BIGGER CUT.

IN THE MEANTIME, WE'RE CHECKING EVERYONE'S PROGRESS--SEEING IF THERE'S ANYTHING *WE* CAN DO TO HELP.

YEAH, *YOU* CAN *HELP*--YOU CAN HELP BY STAYING OUT OF OUR WAY. THE LAST THING WE NEED IS INTERFERENCE FROM CORPORATE PAPER-PUSHERS.

I'M SORRY ABOUT THE WAY ACKLAND TREATED YOU--

DON'T BE. HE HAD EVERY RIGHT. I *NOW* WHAT KIND OF A BITCH I'VE BEEN--

--WOW.

WHAT'S THE MATTER?

OH--YOU HAVEN'T GOTTEN OUT MUCH SINCE YOU ARRIVED, HAVE YOU?

MY JOB... MY *LIFE* TO THAT POINT HAD BEEN CONCERNED WITH SCHEDULES AND NUMBERS AND QUARTERLY REPORTS -- A FULL, SATISFYING LIFE -- I *THOUGHT.* SEE-ING THE SUNSET THAT DAY, I SUDDENLY REALIZED HOW *MUCH* I'D BEEN MISSING.

LITTLE DID I KNOW THAT WOULD BE THE *LAST* TIME I'D EVER VIEW A SUNDOWN WITH ANY EMOTION OTHER THAN *DREAD.*

"GEO-SYNCHRONOUS ORBIT IN FIVE HOURS. CHECK ON CHX."

"THERE'S SOME FLUTTER, BUT WE'RE COMPENSATING -- WE CAN DECOUPLE ANYTIME AFTER ORBIT IS ACHIEVED. THEN IT'S --

"-- HEL-LO, *RYUSHI!* JESUS, WHAT A DUST-BALL."

SHIT, *TOM* -- WHAT KIND OF MOUTH-BREATHER WOULD WANT TO MOVE ALL THE WAY OUT TO THIS *HELL-HOLE* -- ESPECIALLY WHEN THERE'S LAND AVAILABLE ON NOVA-TERRA?

I DON'T KNOW, *SCOTT.* BUT I'LL JUST BET YOU --

"-- RYUSHI IS *SOMEBODY'S* IDEA OF PARADISE."

HERE SHE COMES! NOW IT'S *REALLY* GONNA HIT THE FAN...

THIS MESSAGE JUST ARRIVED FOR YOU, MS. NOGUCHI--

IT'S FROM THE SHUTTLE *MASUKO-MARU*--

"E.T.A. SEVEN STANDARD EARTH DAYS...*SHIGERU CHIGUSA* ON BOARD-- COMING TO INSPECT THE OPERATION *PERSONALLY*..."?

MR. CHIGUSA'S SON... COMING *HERE*...?

THEY SAY THAT TROUBLE COMES IN *THREES*--

SCREECH

WE HAD A LONG NIGHT AHEAD OF US. I HOPED THE *NEXT* TWO DISASTERS WOULD AT LEAST WAIT UNTIL MORNING.

I GOT YOUR MESSAGE, ROTH. WHAT'S THE PROBLEM?

TAKE A LOOK, MR. ACKLAND.

IT WAS A VAIN HOPE. THE 'TERROR' WAS ALREADY IN OUR MIDST-- WE JUST DIDN'T KNOW IT YET.

CHRIST! WHAT THE *HELL* IS IT?

BESIDES UGLIER THAN SHIT? I WAS HOPING *YOU* COULD TELL *ME*.

I'VE NEVER SEEN *ANYTHING* LIKE THESE THINGS. WHERE'D YOU FIND THEM?

UP AT THE HEAD OF BERIKI CANYON. THERE WERE A COUPLE DOZEN OF THEM LYING AROUND DEAD.

THAT'S WHERE WE SCARED UP THESE *POKE-SNOOTS*. THEY WERE STUMBLING AROUND, BUMPING INTO EACH OTHER. THEY ACT LIKE THEY'RE HALF-*ASLEEP*.

MAYBE THEY'RE SICK OR SOMETHIN'--ANYHOW, I THOUGHT YOU SHOULD KNOW.

YOU DID THE RIGHT THING, ROTH.

LOOK, LET'S NOT SPREAD THIS AROUND, OKAY? WE DON'T *KNOW* THAT THERE'S ANYTHING WRONG WITH THE RHYNTH, AND WE DON'T WANT SOME *DICKHEAD* FROM THE COMPANY TO PANIC AND *QUARANTINE* THE WHOLE HERD--

WE'VE GOT TOO MUCH RIDING ON THIS. YOU UNDERSTAND?

YEAH, I UNDERSTAND. WHAT SHOULD I DO WITH *THESE*?

"GIVE THEM TO *DR. REVNA*--BUT TELL HIM YOU FOUND THEM IN *IWA GORGE*. YOU'RE DOING A GREAT JOB, ROTH. THERE'LL BE A *BONUS* FOR YOU WHEN THIS ROUNDUP'S OVER."

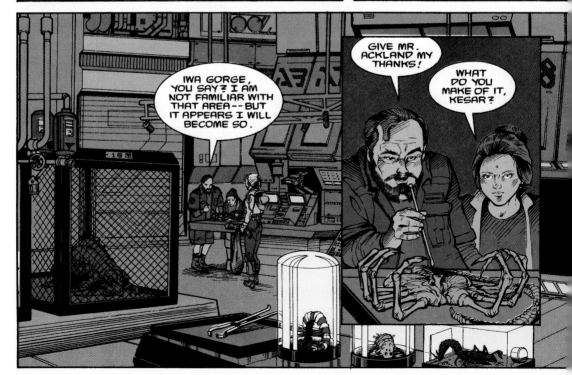

IWA GORGE, YOU SAY? I AM NOT FAMILIAR WITH THAT AREA--BUT IT APPEARS I WILL BECOME SO.

GIVE MR. ACKLAND MY THANKS!

WHAT DO YOU MAKE OF IT, KESAR?

I BEAMED A MESSAGE TO THE HOME OFFICE EXPRESSING MY PLEASURE AT THE NEWS OF SHIGERU CHIGUSA'S VISIT *AND* MY REQUEST FOR A BETTER PRICE FOR THE RANCHERS-- SUPPORTING IT WITH A NEW, *STEPPED-UP* SCHEDULE FOR THE HARVEST. THEN I GRABBED SIX HOURS OF SLEEP BEFORE GOING OUT TO MAKE *SURE* WE COULD KEEP MY PROMISE.

A *PARTY*?! IS THIS *REALLY* NECESSARY?

PROSPERITY WELLS
HOMES LECTOR CREW

I *TOLD* YOU-- YOU CAN'T RUN PEOPLE LIKE MACHINES. YOU THINK THE PAST THREE YEARS ON THIS ROCK HAVE BEEN EASY FOR THESE FOLKS? THIS IS THEIR FIRST ROUNDUP-- EVERYTHING THEY'VE BEEN *WORKING* FOR!

IF THEY WANT TO CELEBRATE THEIR ACCOMPLISHMENT, *LET THEM!* OTHERWISE, SHIGERU HIGUSA WILL ARRIVE JUST IN TIME TO WITNESS A FULL-SCALE *REVOLT!*

YOU'RE RIGHT-- *AGAIN*, HIROKI.

COME ON, LET'S GO *GREET* THE SHIP-- IT'S DUE ANY MINUTE.

IT WAS IMPOSSIBLE NOT TO GET CAUGHT UP IN THE EXCITEMENT OF THE MOMENT. CHILDREN WERE LAUGHING... HUSBANDS AND WIVES WERE ACTING LIKE YOUNG LOVERS... SOMEONE FED MUSIC OVER THE PUBLIC ADDRESS SYSTEM.

OH, THE HOME OFFICE CALLED-- THEY *APPROVED* THE PRICE HIKE FOR THE RANCHERS. I HAVEN'T TOLD ANYONE-- I FIGURED YOU'D WANT THE PLEASURE.

GOOD, I CAN'T WAIT TO SEE ACKLAND'S FACE.

UP HERE. THE ANTENNA TOWER IS THE *ONLY* PLACE TO WATCH A LANDING.

CAN IT SUPPORT *BOTH* OF US?

LET'S FIND OUT.

KEEP CLEAR

300 LB WEIGHT LIMIT

FOR A MOMENT I WAS ABLE TO FORGET MY JOB--

--FORGET EVERYTHING BUT PLEASANT MEMORIES... OF MYSELF AS A LITTLE GIRL... OF *OBON* FESTIVALS WITH MY PARENTS...

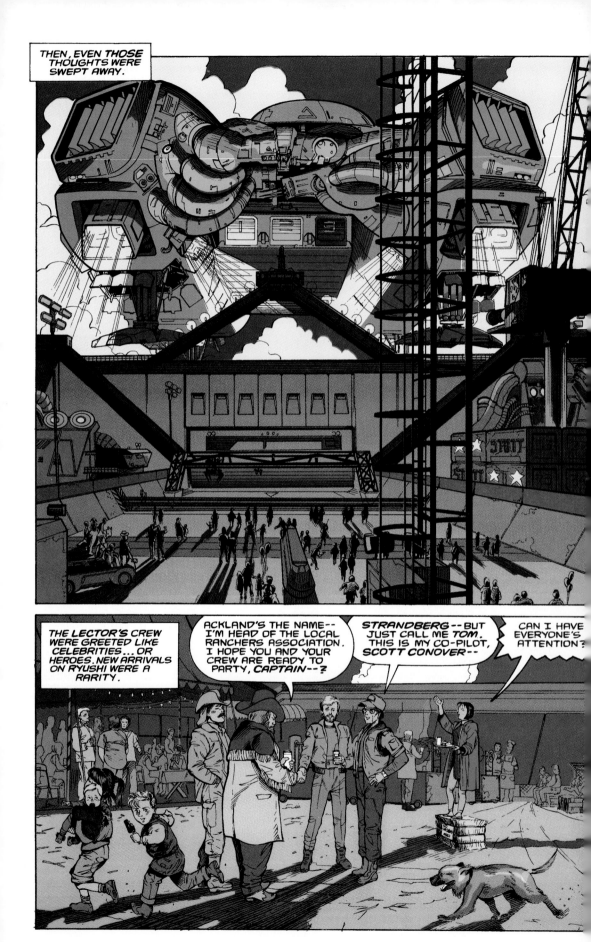

THEN, EVEN THOSE THOUGHTS WERE SWEPT AWAY.

THE *LECTOR'S* CREW WERE GREETED LIKE CELEBRITIES... OR HEROES. NEW ARRIVALS ON RYUSHI WERE A RARITY.

ACKLAND'S THE NAME-- I'M HEAD OF THE LOCAL RANCHERS ASSOCIATION. I HOPE YOU AND YOUR CREW ARE READY TO PARTY, *CAPTAIN--*?

STRANDBERG--BUT JUST CALL ME *TOM*. THIS IS MY CO-PILOT, *SCOTT CONOVER--*

CAN I HAVE EVERYONE'S ATTENTION?

I KNOW YOU'RE ALL ANXIOUS TO BEGIN THE FESTIVITIES, BUT FIRST, I HAVE AN IMPORTANT ANNOUNCEMENT!

WHO'S THE BABE?

YOU MEAN BITCH.

LOADING WILL PROCEED AS FOLLOWS--ACKLAND, YOU'RE FIRST ON DECK. HARRISON'S NEXT, FOLLOWED BY LUCCINI AND MARIANETTI.

OH, ONE MORE THING-- THE COMPANY GAVE THEIR ANSWER ON THE PRICE ADJUSTMENT--

--YOU'LL BE GETTING THE INCREASE YOU REQUESTED.

ENJOY THE PARTY, EVERY- ONE.

GOOD JOB, MACHIKO!

I WAS DOING A GOOD JOB-- BUT ONE DAY DIDN'T UNDO SIX MONTHS OF STUPIDITY.

FOR THE RANCHERS, WATCHING THE SULLEN, PLODDING COLUMNS OF RHYNTH BOARD THE LECTOR WAS THE CULMINATION OF YEARS OF HARD WORK.

EVERY LUMBERING STEP, EVERY NERVOUS SNORT, MEANT MORE CREDITS IN THEIR ACCOUNT...

ZZZT

THE RANCHERS AND THEIR FAMILIES HAD REASON TO CELEBRATE, BUT THE BUSTLE AND COMMOTION FILLED ME WITH MELANCHOLY.

PERHAPS IT WAS THE SORROWFUL BRAYING OF THE RHYNTH THAT GOT TO ME... OR MAYBE IT WAS SIMPLY THE KNOWLEDGE THAT WITH THIS FIRST PHASE OF COLONIZATION COMPLETED, HIROKI WOULD BE LEAVING.

I'D NEVER EXPECTED MUCH FROM HIM--AFTER ALL, I WAS TAKING OVER HIS JOB. BUT HE HADN'T LET THAT AFFECT HIS PROFESSIONAL-ISM--OR OUR RELATIONSHIP.

DN-3Q

C'MON! MOVE IT, LARD-ASS!

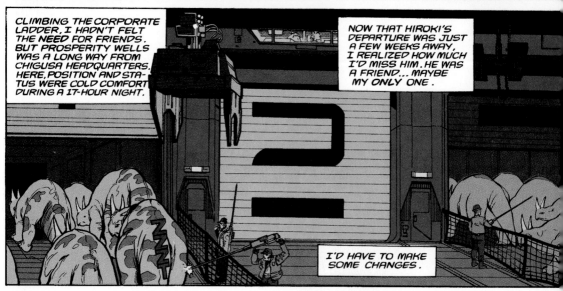

CLIMBING THE CORPORATE LADDER, I HADN'T FELT THE NEED FOR FRIENDS. BUT PROSPERITY WELLS WAS A LONG WAY FROM CHIGUSA HEADQUARTERS. HERE, POSITION AND STA-TUS WERE COLD COMFORT DURING A 17-HOUR NIGHT.

NOW THAT HIROKI'S DEPARTURE WAS JUST A FEW WEEKS AWAY, I REALIZED HOW MUCH I'D MISS HIM. HE WAS A FRIEND... MAYBE MY ONLY ONE.

I'D HAVE TO MAKE SOME CHANGES.

REALLY? THANKS, MS. NOGUCHI.

GO JOIN THE PARTY, COLLINS-- I'LL WATCH THINGS HERE.

IT'S JUST 'MACHIKO' FROM NOW ON, COLLINS, OKAY?

ER...OKAY. OH, WHEN DOC REVNA GETS BACK, TELL HIM THE HOME OFFICE RECEIVED HIS REPORT. IT'S IN THE TRAY WITH HIS NOTES.

"GETS BACK? FROM WHERE?"

"A COUPLE OF HOURS AGO HE SIGNED OUT FOR A HOVER BIKE-- SAID HE WAS GOING UP TO IWA GORGE TO LOOK FOR SOMETHING."

"IWA GORGE? I WONDER WHAT HE'S LOOKING FOR UP THERE?"

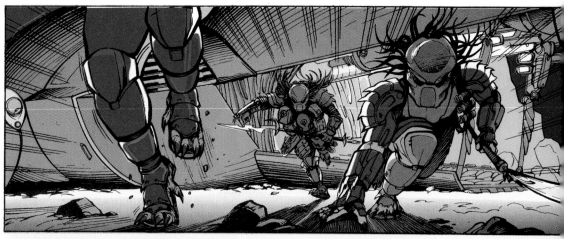

I SCANNED THE REPORT REVNA HAD BEAMED TO EARTH. MOST OF IT WENT BEYOND THE BASIC XT-BIOLOGY COURSES I HAD IN SCHOOL--

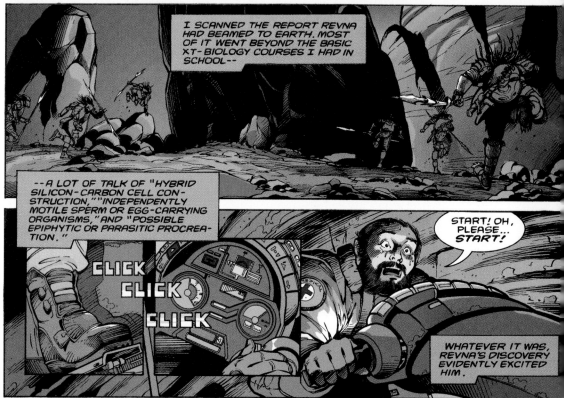

--A LOT OF TALK OF "HYBRID SILICON-CARBON CELL CON-STRUCTION," "INDEPENDENTLY MOTILE SPERM OR EGG-CARRYING ORGANISMS," AND "POSSIBLE EPIPHYTIC OR PARASITIC PROCREA-TION."

CLICK CLICK CLICK

START! OH, PLEASE... START!

WHATEVER IT WAS, REVNA'S DISCOVERY EVIDENTLY EXCITED HIM.

CLIC...

VA-ROOM

WHOOSH

58

I PUNCHED UP A MAP OF THE IWA GORGE AREA.

THUD

SLAM

NOTHING BUT ROCKS AND SAND...

...AND A MAZE OF NARROW GULLIES AND BOX CANYONS.

ROAR

IT SEEMED AN UNLIKELY PLACE TO LOOK FOR ANYTHING--

YAAAH!

WHAM

--ESPECIALLY SOMETHING LIVING.

BUT REVNA WAS A SMART MAN--PROBABLY SMARTER THAN ANYONE ELSE ON RYUSHI--

--IF HE WAS LOOKING FOR SOMETHING IN IWA GORGE, THAT MUST BE THE PLACE TO LOOK FOR IT.

I LIKED THE DOC--

CRUNCH

The disparity in ratio between the smooth-backed specimens and the single carcass with dorsal spines notwithstanding, I believe the differences between the two types represent --

-- sexual indicators—not of the specimens themselves—but of the zygote or "egg" that each carries. As stated above, none of the specimens is equipped for independent life --

-- their sole purpose seems to be nothing more than that of a living delivery vehicle—an "ambulatory penis," if you will. While it is risky to postulate too much from such a tiny sam-

"AMBULATORY PENIS," HUH? CONJURES UP QUITE AN *IMAGE*, DOESN'T IT?

YOU'RE *DRUNK*.

YEAH, BUT NOT *TOO* DRUNK-- *IF* YOU KNOW WHAT I MEAN, MS. NOGUSHI.

IT'S NOGU-CHI-- BUT YOU CAN CALL ME MA'AM.

YEAH? I HEARD ABOUT WHAT A NUT-BUSTER YOU ARE. TOUGH LADY. COMPANY RAMROD.

WELL, I GOT YOUR *RAM-ROD*-- RIGHT *HERE*.

SCOTT?

AAH!

64

CRASH

UFF!

THESE DOORS
(MUST BE CLOSED)

E 501
E 502
SHUTDOWN

YOU NEXT?

NO, *NO!* I WAS JUST COMING TO TELL YOU THAT THE SHIP IS LOADED AND THAT WE'LL BE MAKING OUR FIRST SHUTTLE RUN--

AS SOON AS THE IN-SPECTORS GIVE YOUR *CRITTERS* A CLEAN BILL OF HEALTH.

CARGO STAR

BETTER HAVE THEM CHECK *THIS* CRITTER, TOO, CAPTAIN--

ESPECIALLY HIS *JUDGMENT.*

YEAH, HE'S THE DESIGNATED DRINKER THIS RUN--TOMORROW IT'LL BE *MY* TURN.

YOUR TURN TO *DRINK*--OR YOUR TURN TO GET SOME OF WHAT *I* GAVE *HIM*?

UH, LOOK, I'LL MAKE SURE HE DOESN'T BOTHER YOU AGAIN--OKAY?

EXIT

OP

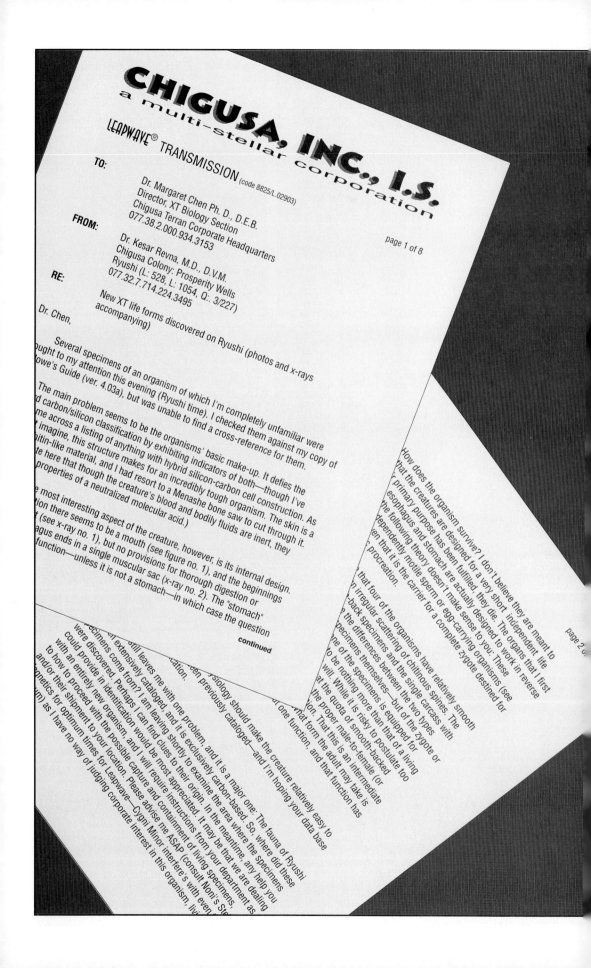

CHIGUSA, INC., I.S.
a multi-stellar corporation

LEAPWAVE® TRANSMISSION (code 8825/L.02903)

TO: Dr. Margaret Chen Ph. D., D.E.B.
Director, XT Biology Section
Chigusa Terran Corporate Headquarters
077.38.2.000.934.3153

FROM: Dr. Kesar Revna, M.D., D.V.M.
Chigusa Colony: Prosperity Wells
Ryushi (L: 528, L: 1054, Q:. 3/227)
077.32.7.714.224.3495

RE: New XT life forms discovered on Ryushi (photos and x-rays accompanying)

Dr. Chen,

Several specimens of an organism of which I'm completely unfamiliar were brought to my attention this evening (Ryushi time). I checked them against my copy of Lowe's Guide (ver. 4.03a), but was unable to find a cross-reference for them.

The main problem seems to be the organisms' basic make-up. It defies the ...d carbon/silicon classification by exhibiting hybrid indicators of both—though I've ...me across a listing of anything with hybrid silicon-carbon cell construction. As ...t imagine, this structure makes for an incredibly tough organism. The skin is a ...hitin-like material, and I had resort to a Menashe bone saw to cut through it. ...te here that though the creature's blood and bodily fluids are inert, they ...properties of a neutralized molecular acid.)

...e most interesting aspect of the creature, however, is its internal design. ...tion there seems to be a mouth (see x-ray no. 1), but no provisions for thorough digestion or ...agus ends in a single muscular sac (x-ray no. 2). The "stomach" ...function—unless it is not a stomach—in which case the question

continued

How does the organism survive? I don't believe they are meant to ...hat the creatures are designed for a very short, independent life. ...primary purpose has been fulfilled, they die. The organs that I first ...esophagus and stomach are actually designed to work in reverse ...the following theory doesn't make sense to you: These ...ependently, motile sperm or egg-carrying organisms (see ...en that it is the carrier for a complete zygote destined for ...procreation.

...that four of the organisms have relatively smooth ...n irregular scattering of chitinous spines. The ...back specimens and the single carcass with ...the differences between the two types ...e the specimens themselves—but of the zygote or ...o be nothing more than that of a living ...will. While it is risky to postulate too ...at the quota of smooth-backed ...the proper male-to-female (or ...on. That this is an intermediate ...that form the adult may take is ...on, and that function has

...still leaves me with one problem, and it is a major one. The fauna of Ryushi
...ecimens come from? I am leaving shortly to examine the area where the specimens
...were discovered. Perhaps I can find clues to their origin. In the meantime, any help you
...could provide in identification would be most appreciated. It may be that we are dealing
...with an entirely new organism, and I will require instructions from your department as
...to how to proceed with the possible capture and containment of living specimens,
...and/or their shipment to your location. Please advise me ASAP (consult Noni's Ste...
...getics for optimum times for Leapwave—Cygni Minor interfere's with even...
...m) as I have no way of judging corporate interest in this organism, livi...

...extensively cataloged, and it is exclusively carbon-based. So, where did these
...been previously cataloged—and I'm hoping your data base
...ysiology should make the creature relatively easy to
...at one function, and that function has

DAMN BITCH--

SHE CAN'T TREAT ME LIKE THAT--

YEAH? MAYBE YOU WANT TO GO BACK AND TELL *HER* THAT--

WHAT'S WITH THE *LIGHTS*? PRINDLE'S TEAM IS GETTING SLOPPY-- THE MAINTENANCE ON THIS TUB HAS GONE TO HELL!

CLICK CLICK CLICK

CLICK CLICK KLANK!

HANG ON A SEC. LET ME GRAB A LIGHT.

SURE. BUT YOU KNOW WHAT I MEAN-- I'M A GODDAMNED *STAR-PILOT!*

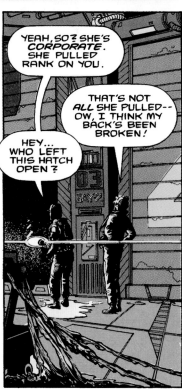

YEAH, SO? SHE'S *CORPORATE.* SHE PULLED RANK ON YOU.

THAT'S NOT ALL SHE PULLED-- OW, I THINK MY BACK'S BEEN BROKEN!

HEY... WHO LEFT THIS HATCH OPEN?

WELL, THAT ACKLAND GUY *WARNED* YOU... JESUS, THE FLOOR'S ALL STICKY...

BUT *YOU* WOULDN'T LISTEN TO HIM. *NO--* YOU HAD TO GO MESS WITH THE QUEEN...

...BEE.

SLAM!

chapter

5

"WE'VE GOT AN EMERGENCY HERE"

**CHIGUSA CORP'S
RYUSHI COLONY
PROSPERITY WELLS**

1. Chigusa Corp. offices and Op Center, Community Center, mess hall, and living quarters for Chigusa employees.

2. Heavy equipment storage and mechanic's crane.

3. Main garage.

4. Abatoir and local holding pens (for food).

5. Powerhouse and sewage treatment plant.

6. Main well and pumping station.

7. Pre-loading pen.

8. Loading ramps.

9. Spacecraft cargo doors and shield wall to protect complex from spacecraft's engine wash.

10. Container storage and main loading crane.

11. School and Recreation Center (includes theater and mini-sports arena, baseball diamond and soccer field).

12. Main transmitting antenna.

13. "Little Earth" shopping complex.

14. Med Center and heli-pad.

15. Quarantine pens.

16. Holding pens.

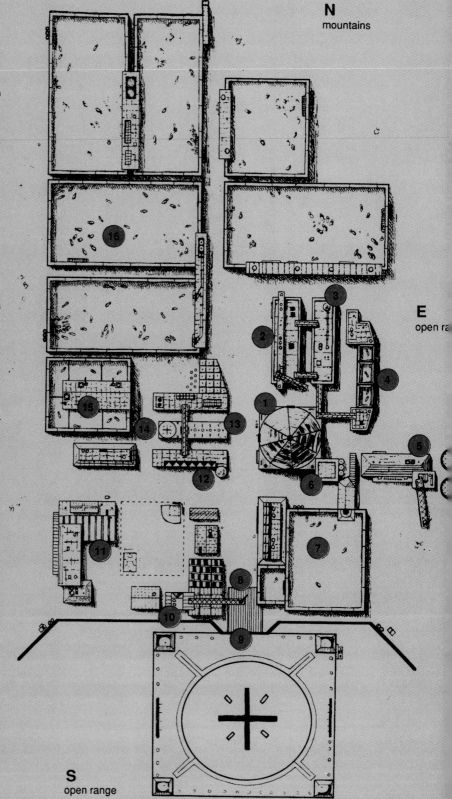

DOUBLE SUNS BLAZED UPON PROSPERITY WELLS... BANISHED THE SHADOWS... DRIED MEN'S SWEAT TO A CHAFING, SALTY CRUST... ERASED EVEN THE **MEMORY** OF COMFORT.

AS "BIG" CYGNI AND "LITTLE" CYGNI CREPT TOWARD THEIR ZENITHS, ACTIVITY ON THE GROUND SLOWED--

--UNTIL EVERYTHING THAT LIVED BECAME AS STILL AS THE THIN, BREATHLESS AIR.

No...

MACHIKO?

CLICK

No-- Huh... WHA--?

MACHIKO... ARE YOU AWAKE?

WHAT TIME IS IT?

ALMOST NOON. LOOK, I KNOW YOU WERE UP LATE LAST NIGHT, BUT--

IT'S AWFULLY WARM IN HERE, ISN'T IT?

--DOC REVNA STILL HASN'T RETURNED, AND Mrs. DOC IS GETTING PSYCHED. I'VE SENT OUT A CREW IN THE COPTER TO SEARCH FOR HIM--

--BUT I THOUGHT IT WOULD BE BEST IF THE STAFF SAW THAT YOU WERE IN ON THIS, TOO.

YOU'RE RIGHT, HIROKI. GIVE ME TWO MINUTES TO GET DRESSED.

DAY 12

DRS. KESAR & MIRIAM REVNA, MD, DVM, DE MEDICAL

OFFICE ENTRANCE

Mrs. DOC WANTED TO CHECK OUT A HOVER BIKE AND GO LOOKING FOR HIM ON HER OWN, BUT I THOUGHT--

--WHY RISK HAVING *BOTH* OF THEM LOST OUT THERE?

RIGHT.

Oh, Ms. NOGUCHI-- DID THEY FIND MY KESAR?

NOT YET, Dr. REVNA, BUT WE'VE GOT OUR BEST PEOPLE OUT LOOKING FOR HIM.

IS THERE ANYTHING YOU CAN THINK OF THAT MIGHT HELP US LOCATE YOUR HUSBAND? SOMETHING YOU MIGHT NOT HAVE THOUGHT WAS IMPORTANT BEFORE?

NO--NO, I DON'T THINK SO. KESAR WAS ON HIS WAY UP TO IWA GORGE--

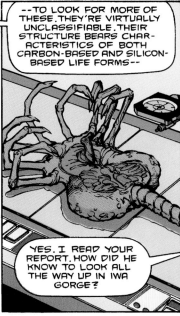

--TO LOOK FOR MORE OF THESE. THEY'RE VIRTUALLY UNCLASSIFIABLE. THEIR STRUCTURE BEARS CHARACTERISTICS OF BOTH CARBON-BASED AND SILICON-BASED LIFE FORMS--

YES. I READ YOUR REPORT. HOW DID HE KNOW TO LOOK ALL THE WAY UP IN IWA GORGE?

THAT'S WHERE SHE SAID SHE FOUND THEM.

"SHE"?

YES... WHAT'S HER NAME? THE YOUNG WOMAN WHO WORKS FOR *FLYING "A"*... ROTH.

WHAT WOULD ROTH BE DOING ALL THE WAY UP IN IWA GORGE? ACKLAND DOESN'T HAVE ANY HERDS WITHIN TWENTY KLIKS OF THERE.

THOSE THINGS *WEREN'T FOUND* IN IWA GORGE.

Huh?

THINK ABOUT IT. IF YOU WERE ACKLAND AND YOU DISCOVERED SOME NEW LIFE FORM THE NIGHT BEFORE YOUR RHYNTH WERE TO BE SHIPPED OFF-PLANET, WOULD *YOU* RISK HAVING YOUR ENTIRE YEAR'S PROFITS HELD UP IN QUARANTINE?

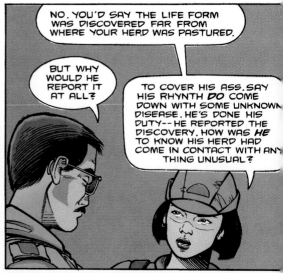

NO. YOU'D SAY THE LIFE FORM WAS DISCOVERED FAR FROM WHERE YOUR HERD WAS PASTURED.

BUT WHY WOULD HE REPORT IT AT ALL?

TO COVER HIS ASS. SAY HIS RHYNTH *DO* COME DOWN WITH SOME UNKNOWN DISEASE. HE'S DONE HIS DUTY-- HE REPORTED THE DISCOVERY. HOW WAS *HE* TO KNOW HIS HERD HAD COME IN CONTACT WITH ANYTHING UNUSUAL?

SO WHAT'S OUR NEXT MOVE?

WE TALK TO ROTH FIRST, THEN ACKLAND. IF ANYTHING HAS HAPPENED TO REVNA, HE'LL PAY.

HE SENT REVNA ON A WILD GOOSE CHASE--

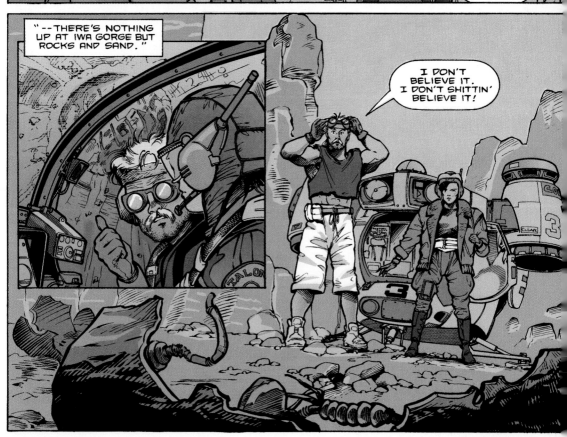

"--THERE'S NOTHING UP AT IWA GORGE BUT ROCKS AND SAND."

I DON'T BELIEVE IT. I DON'T SHITTIN' BELIEVE IT!

76

LOOK AT THIS, IKEDA! DO YOU KNOW WHAT THIS IS? THIS IS AN HONEST-TO-GOD ALIEN SPACESHIP--OR WHAT'S LEFT OF IT.

THIS WASN'T BUILT IN DETROIT, OR OSAKA, OR EVEN SEOUL. WE'RE TALKIN' *UFOs* -- CHARIOTS OF THE GODS!

THINK OF THE NEW INFORMATION! IF WE CAN FIGURE OUT WHAT MADE THIS THING TICK--

WHY NOT JUST ASK *HIM*?

WHA--?

HOLY--! WHEREVER HE CAME FROM, THEY GROW 'EM *BIG*!

I THINK HE'S DEAD--

--NO! HE'S STILL BREATHING.

THIS IS TOO SHITTIN' UN-BELIEVABLE! I MEAN--

CAN IT, SPANNER. HELP ME GET HIM INTO THE COPTER.

SAY AGAIN, COPTER-1-- YOU FOUND *WHAT*?

NEVER MIND. YOU'LL SEE IT WHEN WE GET BACK.

NO SIGN OF THE DOC ANYWHERE-- BUT WHAT WE'VE FOUND CAN'T WAIT. COPTER-1 RETURNING TO BASE. IKEDA OUT.

"HELP HER," SHE SAYS. THIS GUY WEIGHS A SHITTIN' TON...

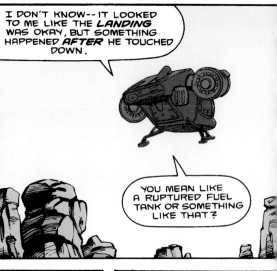

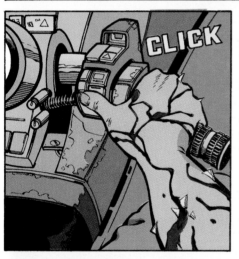

YOU'RE IN A LOT OF TROUBLE, Ms. ROTH. IF ANYTHING HAS HAPPENED TO Dr. REVNA, YOU'LL BE HELD RESPONSIBLE.

BUT THAT'S NOTHING COMPARED TO THE CHARGES YOU'LL FACE IF FLYING "A" CARCASSES INFECTED WITH DANGEROUS BACTERIA OR VIRUS END UP ON EARTH.

BUT IT'S NOT MY FAULT-- I WAS JUST FOLLOWING ORDERS. Mr. ACKLAND TOLD ME TO--

HEY, NOGUCHI!-- I THOUGHT A MAN HAD A RIGHT TO BE PRESENT WHEN HIS ACCUSERS WERE TESTIFYING AGAINST HIM.

OR WERE YOU PLANNING TO TRY ME IN ABSENTIA? NO-- THAT COULDN'T BE IT-- YOU NEED A JUDGE TO HOLD A TRIAL. I HAVEN'T SEEN ANY JUDGES WANDERING AROUND PROSPERITY WELLS, HAVE YOU?

YOU'VE VIOLATED COMPANY POLICY AND JEOPARDIZED THE SECURITY OF THIS COMPLEX AND ITS PERSONNEL, ACKLAND. I FIGURE THAT'S ALL THE LEGAL AUTHORITY I NEED.

"FRONTIER JUSTICE," EH? YOU REALLY THINK YOU'VE GOT THE BACKING TO MAKE CHARGES STICK? IN CASE YOU HAVEN'T NOTICED, Ms. NOGUCHI, YOU AREN'T EXACTLY THE MOST POPULAR PERSON IN THIS SETTLEMENT.

YOU'RE RIGHT-- I'M JUST THE NEW BOSS. BUT DOC REVNA HAS BEEN HERE SINCE THE BEGINNING-- TREATING THE RANCHERS' STOCK, TREATING THEIR FAMILIES--

--DELIVERING THEIR BABIES. SO FAR, THE DOC'S JUST LISTED AS MISSING. BUT IF HE TURNS UP DEAD, WHO DO YOU THINK FOLKS ARE GOING TO SIDE WITH: YOU-- OR HIS GRIEVING WIDOW?

LOOK, I DIDN'T EXPECT THE DOC TO GO OUT LOOKING FOR *MORE* OF THOSE THINGS--

BUT IF HE DID, YOU WANTED TO MAKE SURE HE LOOKED IN THE *WRONG* PLACE.

WE HAD NO WAY OF KNOWING WHETHER THOSE RHYNTH WERE INFECTED OR NOT! I DIDN'T WANT TO DELAY THE WHOLE OPERATION--

DIDN'T IT OCCUR TO YOU THAT *TROUBLE* WITH *YOUR* HERD COULD BE THE REASON THE LECTOR'S *STILL* PARKED OUT THERE?

WHAT?! I DON'T BELIEVE IT!

I MEANT TO TELL YOU, BUT WITH EVERYTHING THAT'S BEEN HAPPENING...

THOSE RHYNTH ARE GOING TO BE HELL TO MANAGE AFTER STANDING IN THE SUNS ALL DAY!

0:OPERATIONS-
►COLLINS◄

CLICK CLICK

COLLINS! WHY HASN'T THE LECTOR TAKEN ITS FIRST LOAD BACK TO ITS ORBITER?

I COULDN'T SAY, MA'AM. WE'VE BEEN TRYING TO CONTACT THEM ALL DAY, BUT THEY DON'T RESPOND.

THEN SEND SOMEONE OUT THERE TO TALK TO THEM IN PERSON!

I'LL GO *MYSELF.*

GOOD. DON'T WASTE YOUR TIME WITH *CONOVER--* TALK TO *STRANDBERG.*

85

"REMIND HIM THAT WE'RE ON A TIGHT SCHEDULE."

OH, JESUS... SCOTT... ARE YOU... CAN YOU HEAR ME?

WHAT HAPPENED TO US...? ARE THEY--?

AGHH!

OH, GOD--

...THE COMPANY HAS MILLIONS INVESTED--

Ms. NOGUCHI, REPORT TO THE MED CENTER-- IMMEDIATELY! Ms. NOGUCHI TO THE MED CENTER!

INCOMING MESSAGE
NOGUCHI-MACHIKO MSS

YOU'D BETTER PRAY THEY'VE FOUND REVNA, ACKLAND!

WEST

FOUR CRACKED RIBS AND EXTENSIVE CONTUSIONS IN THE DORSAL REGION.

HEY, Ms. NOGUCHI! LOOK WHAT WE FOUND!

THE SPECIMEN APPEARS TO BREATHE A MIXTURE OF METHANE WITH TRACES OF OTHER COMMON ELEMENTS...

SO MUCH FOR QUARAN- TINE...

A CHANCE ENCOUNTER WITH INTELLIGENT XTs WAS CON- SIDERED SO REMOTE THAT THE COMPANY'S OFF-PLANET MANUAL CONTAINED ONLY ONE LINE ON THE SUBJECT:

"AVOID DIRECT CONTACT UNTIL SPECIALLY TRAINED PERSONNEL ARRIVE ON THE SCENE."

WE WERE ABOUT TO WRITE A WHOLE NEW CHAPTER.

NO. THIS CREATURE HAS A COMPLETELY DIFFERENT CELL STRUCTURE. I WISH KESAR WERE HERE-- HE COULD TELL US MORE.

QUITE AN ARSENAL. THIS GUY'S NO EXPLORER. THIS IS STUFF YOU'D PACK FOR A HUNTING TRIP... OR AN *INVASION*.

I DON'T THINK THIS IS HIS FIRST TRIP TO RYUSHI, EITHER. I CAN'T PLACE THE REST OF THIS STUFF, BUT THIS STRAP IS *DEFINITELY* RHYNTH-HIDE!

BUT IF THIS GUY--OR OTHERS LIKE HIM HAVE BEEN HERE BEFORE, WHY HAVEN'T WE SEEN ANY SIGN OF THEM? AND DO THEY HAVE ANYTHING TO DO WITH THE CRITTERS ACKLAND'S PEOPLE FOUND?

THIS IS FAMILIAR...I'VE SEEN IT SOME-WHERE...

WAS IT A DREAM? IT WAS DARK... AND HOT--

LOOK OUT! STOP!

WHAT NOW--?

CRASH

WHAT HAPPENED?

IT'S THE SHELDON BOY. CAME RIDING INTO TOWN LIKE A *MANIAC!* WOULDN'T STOP FOR NO ONE UNTIL HE--

MONSTERS!

WHAT'S THAT, SON?

MONSTERS! ≡huff≡ THEY KILLED MOM AND ≡huff≡ DAD! AT FIRST WE COULDN'T *SEE* 'EM, BUT THEN THEY KILLED MY DOG!

I GOT AWAY ≡huff≡ --BUT THEY KILLED MOM AND DAD!

LET'S GET HIM TO THE MED CENTER.

DOC! WE'VE GOT AN *EMERGENCY* HERE!

MONSTERS!

MONSTERS!

I CALLED A TOWN MEETING TO FILL EVERYONE IN ON WHAT WAS HAPPENING.

IT SOUNDED UNBELIEVABLE, EVEN TO ME. BUT, AFTER WE WERE UNABLE TO REACH THEM BY RADIO, I HAD IKEDA DO A FLY-BY OF THE SHELDON RANCH. THE HOUSE WAS IN FLAMES, AND THE FAMILY'S BREEDING STOCK HAD ALL BEEN SLAUGHTERED.

ADD TO THAT OUR "PATIENT" IN THE MED CENTER, AND--

--WE MUST ASSUME AN *ATTACK* IS IMMINENT.

MR. SHIMURA IS IN CHARGE OF SECURITY. ALL ABLE-BODIED PERSONNEL WILL BE EXPECTED TO TAKE A SHIFT ON WATCH. ANYONE NOT ON DUTY WILL REMAIN WITHIN THE MAIN COMPLEX.

THERE IS A THIRTY-THREE-HOUR CURFEW IN EFFECT AS OF NOW.

THE FOLLOWING PERSONNEL WILL REPORT TO ME AT THE END OF THIS MEETING FOR FIRST WATCH...

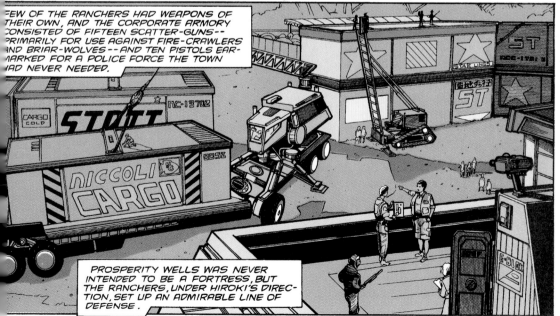

FEW OF THE RANCHERS HAD WEAPONS OF THEIR OWN, AND THE CORPORATE ARMORY CONSISTED OF FIFTEEN SCATTER-GUNS-- PRIMARILY FOR USE AGAINST FIRE-CRAWLERS AND BRIAR-WOLVES -- AND TEN PISTOLS EAR-MARKED FOR A POLICE FORCE THE TOWN HAD NEVER NEEDED.

PROSPERITY WELLS WAS NEVER INTENDED TO BE A FORTRESS, BUT THE RANCHERS, UNDER HIROKI'S DIREC-TION, SET UP AN ADMIRABLE LINE OF DEFENSE.

FACED WITH A COMMON THREAT, THE *RANCHERS* AND THE COM-PANY STAFF COOPERATED AS THEY NEVER HAD BEFORE.

BY TWILIGHT THE WORK WAS FINISHED.

WE DIDN'T KNOW YET THAT THE WORK WAS *IN VAIN.*

MOST EVERYONE'S IN FROM THE OUTLYING RANCHES, Ms. NOGUCHI. TWO DON'T ANSWER OUR SUMMONS-- OUR ONLY *LOCAL* HOLDOUT IS Dr. REVNA. SHE REFUSES TO BE MOVED TO THE MAIN BUILDING.

WE'LL HAVE TO ASSUME OUR ATTACKERS HAVE TAKEN THE TWO RANCHES. AS FOR REVNA, COLLINS IS HER FRIEND-- HAVE *HIM* GO DOWN AND TALK TO HER.

Uh, WE CAN'T FIND COLLINS. NO ONE HAS SEEN HIM SINCE THIS AFTERNOON WHEN YOU SENT HIM OUT TO THE LECTOR--

DO I HAVE TO DO *EVERYTHING* AROUND HERE *MYSELF?* ALL RIGHT-- I'M GOING OUT THERE!

HOLD IT! GOING OUT *WHERE?*

TO *THE LECTOR.* COLLINS HASN'T COME BACK. *I'M* GOING TO FIND OUT WHAT'S GOING ON WITH THEM--

--BUT FIRST I'M GOING TO TRY AND TALK SOME *SENSE* INTO Dr. REVNA.

MACHIKO, IT ISN'T *SAFE...*

WARNING
THESE DOORS MUST BE CLOSED

Okay... I CAN SEE YOU'VE MADE UP YOUR MIND. BUT TAKE THIS. I'LL CALL THE SENTRIES AND LET THEM KNOW YOU'RE ON YOUR WAY.

RIGHT. HAVE WEAVER SET UP THE SAT-LINK WITH EARTH AS SOON AS THE SUNS SET. EXPLAIN OUR SITUATION, AND ASK THEM TO CUT A DEAL FOR MARINE SUPPORT.

A DAY EARLIER THE SPECTACLE OF RYUSHI'S DOUBLE SUNSET HAD STRUCK ME AS BEAUTIFUL.

NOW THE SUNS WINKED MOCKINGLY FROM THE HORIZON -- GLOATING THAT THE PASSAGE OF A SINGLE DAY COULD TRANSFORM PROSPERITY WELLS FROM A PLACE OF CELEBRATION TO AN ARMED CAMP.

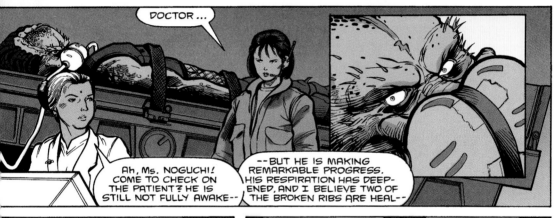

DOCTOR...

Ah, Ms. NOGUCHI! COME TO CHECK ON THE PATIENT? HE IS STILL NOT FULLY AWAKE--

--BUT HE IS MAKING REMARKABLE PROGRESS. HIS RESPIRATION HAS DEEPENED, AND I BELIEVE TWO OF THE BROKEN RIBS ARE HEAL--

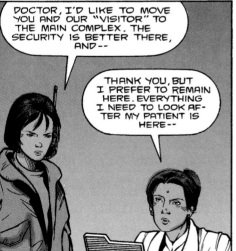

DOCTOR, I'D LIKE TO MOVE YOU AND OUR "VISITOR" TO THE MAIN COMPLEX. THE SECURITY IS BETTER THERE, AND--

THANK YOU, BUT I PREFER TO REMAIN HERE. EVERYTHING I NEED TO LOOK AFTER MY PATIENT IS HERE--

--BESIDES, THIS IS WHERE MY KESAR WILL COME WHEN HE RETURNS. I WILL WAIT HERE FOR HIM.

VERY WELL, DOCTOR. BUT I'M POSTING A GUARD OUTSIDE.

Dr. REVNA WAS FOOLING HERSELF. NO ONE DOUBTED THAT THE DOC HAD MET THE SAME FATE AS THE SHELDONS.

MAYBE WE WERE ALL FOOLING OURSELVES. WE HAD NO WAY OF GUESSING THE ENEMY'S STRENGTH OR INTENTIONS -- NO CLUE AS TO ITS TACTICS OR STRATEGIES.

IN A SENSE, THE INVADERS--IF THAT'S WHAT THEY WERE--HAD **ALREADY** WON. THE MERE FACT OF THEIR EXISTENCE HAD DISRUPTED OUR LIVES AND PUT US ON THE DEFENSIVE.

MED CENTER

HOLDING

HI, RILEY. HI, MASON.

Ms. NOGUCHI-- Mr. SHIMURA SAID YOU WERE COMING. I'M TO ESCORT YOU TO THE LECTOR.

LET ME GUESS, MASON--HIROKI ORDERED YOU TO FOLLOW ME EVEN IF I DECLINED YOUR ESCORT?

YES, MA'AM.

IT WASN'T LIKELY TO ACCOMPLISH MUCH, BUT THE TRIP OUT TO THE LECTOR WAS AT LEAST A POSITIVE ACTION--

WELL, THEN, COME ON.

--IT MADE ME FEEL AS IF WE HADN'T LOST **ALL** OF THE INITIATIVE.

YOU KNOW, I THINK WE'RE WORRYING TOO MUCH. I MEAN, LOOK AT THE SIZE OF THE COMPLEX. YOU'D NEED AN ARMY TO ATTACK THIS PLACE.

Hmm-- SOMEONE LEFT THE DOOR OPEN ...

I THINK THOSE XTs ARE GONNA TAKE ONE LOOK AT PROSPERITY WELLS AND GO BACK HOME.

JUST GIVE ME A SECOND TO GET THE LI--

GAA-AKK!

THE DREAM I'D BEEN UNABLE TO REMEMBER EARLIER CAME BACK TO ME WITH SUDDEN, HORRIFYING CLARITY.

ONLY IT WASN'T A DREAM--

BLAM BLAM BLAM BLAM

--IT WAS A NIGHTMARE--

BLAM BLAM CLIK

--AND IT WAS REAL.

BOOM!

chapter

6

"Never Align Yourself With a Loser"

WE'D DONE OUR BEST, WITH LIMITED PERSONNEL AND RESOURCES, TO FORTIFY PROSPERITY WELLS AGAINST THE "INVADERS." WE COULD HAVE SAVED OURSELVES THE TROUBLE --

-- WE WEREN'T THE *TARGETS* OF THE "INVASION." WE WERE MERELY *BYSTANDERS*, CAUGHT BETWEEN TWO OPPOSING FORCES:

HULKING, HUMANOID WARRIORS LIKE OUR "PATIENT" IN THE MED-CENTER --

-- AND THE SILENT, EYELESS MONSTERS THAT HAUNTED MY DREAMS.

PERHAPS IT WAS THIS CONNECTION TO MY NIGHTMARES -- AS WELL AS THE FACT THAT THE MONSTERS HAD KILLED MASON -- THAT PREDISPOSED ME AGAINST THEM ...

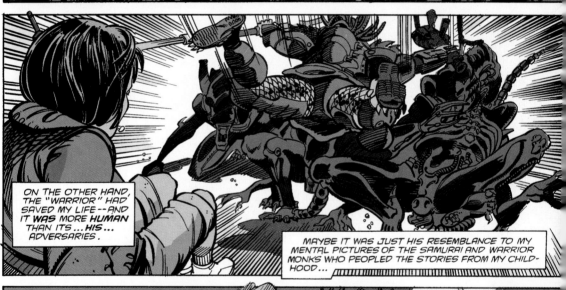

ON THE OTHER HAND, THE "WARRIOR" HAD SAVED MY LIFE -- AND IT *WAS* MORE *HUMAN* THAN ITS ... *HIS* ... ADVERSARIES.

MAYBE IT WAS JUST HIS RESEMBLANCE TO MY MENTAL PICTURES OF THE SAMURAI AND WARRIOR MONKS WHO PEOPLED THE STORIES FROM MY CHILD-HOOD ...

...OR IT COULD HAVE BEEN THAT IT'S SIMPLY HUMAN NATURE TO CHEER FOR THE UNDERDOG.

WHATEVER THE REASON, I CAUGHT MY BREATH AS THE "WARRIOR" LEAPT -- HEROICALLY, IT SEEMED -- INTO BATTLE.

HIS MOVEMENTS WERE SO SWIFT, I COULD SCARCELY FOLLOW THEM...

KLANK

...SO POWERFUL... SO ASSURED...

PLOOM

...SO DEADLY...

THUNK

CHIK

...AND ULTIMATELY FUTILE.

DESPITE HIS SPEED AND STRENGTH AND PRACTICED MOVES, THE "WARRIOR" WAS NOT A **SMART** FIGHTER--

--HE WAS LIKE A **KARATEKA** WHO HAD MASTERED HIS STYLE, BUT HAD NEVER FACED AN OPPONENT IN ACTUAL COMBAT.

HE HAD NOT CHOSEN A "GOOD" FIGHT...

...NOR HAD HE ALLOWED FOR ANY OUTCOME **OTHER** THAN **VICTORY**.

THERE'S A BIG DIFFERENCE BETWEEN HEROISM AND STUPIDITY. IN THE END, THE "WARRIOR" GAINED NOTHING BUT A GLORIOUS--AND POINTLESS--**DEATH**.

I DIDN'T LOOK BACK. I HAD LEARNED A LONG TIME AGO: NEVER ALIGN YOURSELF WITH A LOSER.

...I WAS LISTENING TO HIROKI'S VOICE ON THE COM, THE SOUND OF GUNFIRE ECHOED THROUGH THE STREETS OF THE COMPLEX, MY HEART WAS POUNDING LIKE THUNDER IN MY CHEST--

--AND, SOMEHOW, I HEARD ANOTHER SOUND...OR A *HINT* OF A SOUND: NOTHING MORE THAN AN INTAKE OF BREATH.

IT WASN'T MINE-- AND IT CERTAINLY WASN'T RILEY'S.

FAINT THOUGH IT WAS, IT WAS ENOUGH.

CHUKK

INVISIBILITY. THAT'S HOW THE "WARRIORS" HAD GOTTEN PAST OUR DEFENSES.

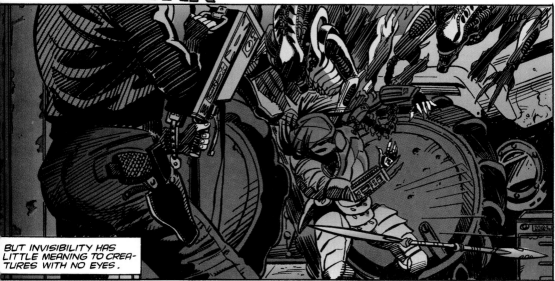

BUT INVISIBILITY HAS LITTLE MEANING TO CREA-TURES WITH NO EYES.

GET READY! SOMETHING'S COMIN'!

DON'T SHOOT! IT'S Ms. NOGUCHI!

DID YOU SEE THEM? HOW MANY DO YOU THINK THERE ARE?

TOO MANY. FALL BACK TO THE INNER DOORS AND GET SOMEONE WITH A WELDING TORCH OVER HERE. SEAL *ALL* OF THE DOORS-- UPPER LEVEL, TOO--EXCEPT THE EAST LOCK. NO ONE GOES IN OR OUT WITHOUT MY AUTHORIZATION.

LOAD THIS FOR ME. AND GET ME SOME EXTRA CLIPS FOR IT.

WILL *THREE* EXTRA CLIPS BE ENOUGH?

MAKE IT FIVE. NO-- TEN.

AND SEAL THOSE DOORS!

DOWNEY, DO YOU HAVE THAT SAT-LINK HOOKED UP YET?

"LITTLE" CYGNI'S STILL INTER- FERING.

WHAT DO YOU HAVE ON THE CAM- ERAS, WEAVER? CAN YOU GET ME A FIX ON HIROKI AND HIS TEAM?

HIROKI AND HIS TEAM HAD GONE OUT AS HEROES. THEY'D SACRIFICED THEMSELVES FOR THE REST OF THE COLONY. BUT I HADN'T BEEN ABLE TO TAKE ADVANTAGE OF THEIR SACRIFICE.

I HAD SQUANDERED THE TIME THEY'D BOUGHT US. I HAD FAILED THE COLONY... AND I HAD FAILED HIROKI.

Ms. NOGUCHI? THIS IS WEAVER. I-- I KNOW YOU AND Mr. SHIMURA WERE FRIENDS. I DON'T MEAN TO INTERRUPT YOU, BUT...

THERE'S SOMETHING YOU SHOULD SEE. I CAN TRANSFER IT TO YOUR SCREEN...

WHAT IS IT, WEAVER?

THIS IS THE FEED FROM THE SECURITY CAMERA ON THE SOUTHWEST SIDE OF THE TOWER. I'VE BOOSTED THE GAIN AS MUCH AS POSSIBLE--

--BUT THE PICTURE'S STILL DARK. A LOT OF THE LIGHTS SEEM TO BE OUT IN THAT SECTION OF THE COMPOUND--

--IT LOOKS LIKE OUR ATTACKERS ARE HAVING A VICTORY CELEBRATION ...

TEN CLIPS! SHE'S NOT THINKIN' OF GOING *OUT* THERE, IS SHE--?

YOU GUESSED IT.

WHO OWNS THE FASTEST HOVER BIKE?

I...I GUESS I DO.

WHERE'S IT PARKED?

EAST LOCK, KEY'S IN THE IGNITION.

THAT'S *IT?* YOU'RE TAKING OFF? WHAT ABOUT THE *REST* OF US? I THOUGHT YOU WERE SUPPOSED TO BE *IN CHARGE*-- WHERE'S YOUR SENSE OF *RESPONSIBILITY?*

SMACK!

RESPONSIBILITY?! HIROKI IS DEAD, AND THIS WHOLE MESS IS *YOUR FAULT*, ACKLAND--

--IF WE LIVE THROUGH THIS, *YOU'RE* GOING TO FIND OUT WHAT HAPPENS TO PEOPLE WHO ARE *RE-SPONSIBLE!*

WEAVER'S IN CHARGE UNTIL I GET BACK, YOU'LL FOLLOW HER ORDERS--*TO THE LETTER*.

DO I MAKE MYSELF *CLEAR?*

SCEEE!

KRIIICH

--SOMETHING THAT WOULD OVER-
WHELM A PERSON AND CLOUD HER
JUDGMENT.

BUT I WAS
IN COMPLETE
CONTROL...

...I KNEW *EXACTLY*
WHAT I WAS DOING.

DR.
REVNA!
I FORGOT
ALL ABOUT
HER!

VREEEEN

DR. REVNA!
IT'S ME--
MACHIKO!

MACHIKO! I
HEARD *SHOOTING*...
IS EVERYTHING
ALL RIGHT?

NO. THINGS
ARE *BAD*-- AND
THEY'RE ABOUT
TO GET *WORSE.*

CAN YOU
HANDLE A
HOVER BIKE,
MIRIAM?

NO, I NEVER
LEARNED. I
ALWAYS RELIED
ON KESAR--

NO GOOD-- I
DON'T HAVE TIME
TO TAKE YOU BACK
TO THE TOWER. OKAY,
LET'S SEE-- DO YOU
KNOW HOW TO USE
ONE OF *THESE?*

111

IT'S A SEMI-AUTOMATIC, SO IT DOES ALL THE WORK *FOR* YOU. JUST AIM IT AT THE BELLY OF WHOMEVER YOU WANT TO SHOOT--AND SQUEEZE THE TRIGGER.

YOU ONLY HAVE SIX ROUNDS-- DON'T WASTE ANY ON WARNING SHOTS.

MS. NOGUCHI-- I AM NOT A SOLDIER...

THIS ISN'T A WAR, MIRIAM. THIS IS *SURVIVAL.*

W-WHO MIGHT I BE SHOOTING AT?

DON'T WORRY-- YOU'LL KNOW WHEN THE TIME COMES

TELL ME, MIRIAM, THE UNCLASSIFIEDS ROTH BROUGHT YOU--KESAR'S REPORT SAID HE THOUGHT THEY MIGHT TRANSMIT EGGS, OR SPORES, TO HOST BODIES.

IS IT POSSIBLE THAT WHEN THOSE SPORES GREW UP, THEY'D LOOK LIKE THIS?

IT IS IMPOSSIBLE TO SAY. WHY DO YOU ASK?

BECAUSE I'VE SEEN SOME OF *THESE* THINGS TONIGHT. THERE WERE DOZENS--MAY-BE *HUNDREDS*-- OF THEM IN THE LECTOR.

I THINK ACKLAND'S RHYNTH WERE INFECTED OR *IMPREGNATED,* BY THESE THINGS, AND THEY SPREAD IT TO ALL OF THE HERDS ON THE SHIP--

--*AND* I THINK OUR TWO UNCLASSI-FIEDS ARE SOMEHOW *CONNECTED.*

WHAT ARE YOU GOING TO DO?

YOU KNOW RHYNTH TEMPERAMENT, RIGHT? I'VE GOT THREE THOU-SAND HEAD THAT HAVE BEEN CRAMMED INTO HOLDING PENS SINCE LAST NIGHT--

--WHAT KIND OF MOOD DO YOU THINK THEY'RE *RIGHT NOW?*

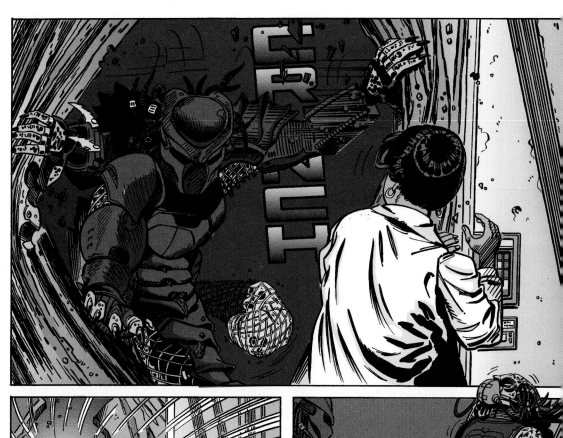

SHING

DON'T EVEN *THINK* ABOUT GETTING UP! YOU GET ONE WARNING-- THEN I *BLOW YOUR HEAD OFF!*

YOU ONLY HAVE SIX ROUNDS--DON'T WASTE ANY ON WARNING SHOTS.

WHA--? THAT'S *MY VOICE...*

MIRIAM! WHAT ARE YOU DOING?

I DON'T THINK HE MEANS US ANY HARM.

THEY *KILLED* HIROKI AND SIX OTHER MEN!

THEY DID-- NOT HIM.

I THINK THIS ONE APPRECIATES OUR HELP. WHEN THE OTHER ONE ATTACKED ME, HE SAVED MY LIFE.

WHAT KIND OF MOOD DO YOU THINK THEY'RE IN *RIGHT NOW?*

C'MON, MIRIAM! WHILE THESE TWO DECIDE WHO'S THE MOST *MACHO*, WE'VE GOT *WORK* TO DO!

THE HOVER BIKE IS TOTALLED--

--WE'LL HAVE TO TAKE THE COPTER.

I DON'T SUPPOSE YOU'RE CHECKED OUT IN A COPTER--?

NO--

-- I ALWAYS RELIED ON KESAR...

YEAH, ME NEITHER. THIS SHOULD BE INTERESTING.

THIS IS NOGUCHI IN COPTER-1-- DO YOU READ ME, TOWER? WHAT'S THE SITUATION THERE?

I READ YOU, COPTER-1. WE'RE ALMOST READY-- BUT YOU SHOULD SEE WHAT'S HAPPEN- ING IN THE SOUTHWEST QUADRANT--

"-- IT LOOKS LIKE ALL-OUT *WAR!*"

AW, CHRIST! WE WERE BETTER OFF IN THE SHIP!

OH... MY... GOD...

WHUP WHUP WHUP

SOUNDS EVEN BETTER THAN I'D HOPED FOR, WEAVER! STAND BY FOR MY SIGNAL!

HANG ON, MIRIAM!

WHERE ARE WE GOING?

WHUP WHUP WHUP

THE HOLDING PENS.

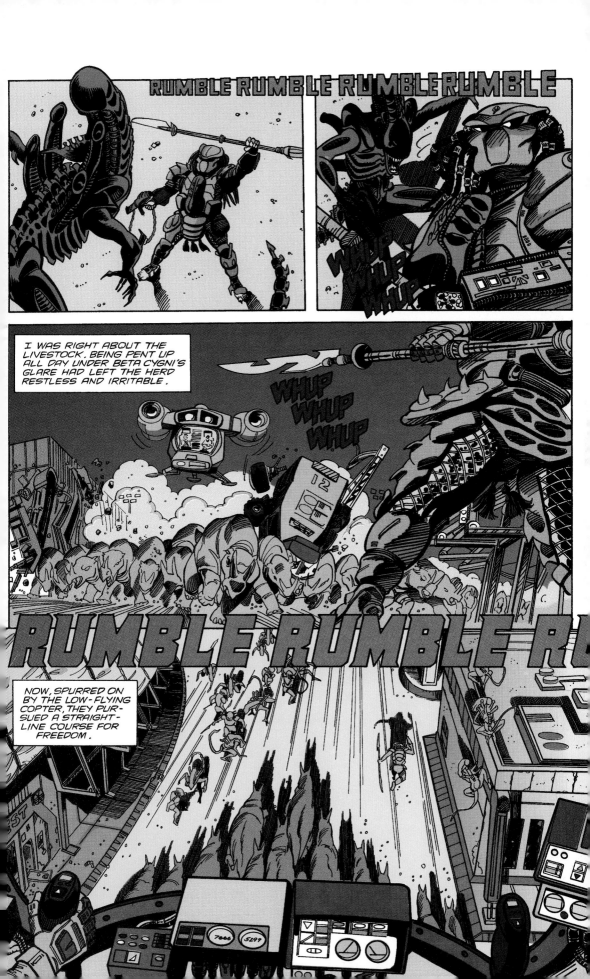

RUMBLE RUMBLE RUMBLE RUMBLE

WHUP WHUP WHUP

I WAS RIGHT ABOUT THE LIVESTOCK. BEING PENT UP ALL DAY UNDER BETA CYGNI'S GLARE HAD LEFT THE HERD RESTLESS AND IRRITABLE.

WHUP WHUP WHUP

RUMBLE RUMBLE RU

NOW, SPURRED ON BY THE LOW-FLYING COPTER, THEY PURSUED A STRAIGHT-LINE COURSE FOR FREEDOM.

THEY SAW EVERYTHING IN THEIR PATH AS AN OBSTACLE TO BE CRUSHED UNDERFOOT.

EVERYTHING.

I COULD HEAR THE THUNDER OF HOOVES AND THE BELLOWING OF THE RHYNTH CLEARLY ABOVE THE POUNDING OF THE COPTER'S BLADES.

I HADN'T TOLD ANYONE BUT WEAVER ABOUT MY PLAN, BUT I HAD TO BELIEVE THAT BY NOW EVERYONE AT THE EAST LOCK HAD FIGURED OUT WHAT WAS HAPPENING.

YOU HEAR THAT RUMBLING? OUR RHYNTH! THAT'S THIS YEAR'S PROFITS GOING DOWN THE TOILET!

WRONG, ACKLAND! THAT'S THE SOUND OF YOUR ASS BEING PULLED OUT OF THE FIRE!

NOW-- GET ON BOARD, OR GET OUT OF THE WAY!

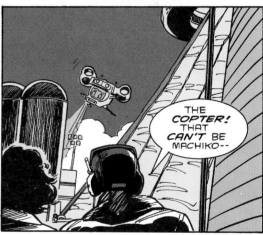

THE COPTER! THAT CAN'T BE MACHIKO--

"--SHE'S NOT LICENSED TO FLY!"

HANG ON, MIRIAM-- I'M GOING TO MAKE ANOTHER PASS!

MACHIKO, LOOK!

"IT'S MY *PATIENT!*"

"WE MUST SAVE HIM!"

ARE YOU *CRAZY?* MIRIAM--THOSE THINGS ARE THE *REASON* WE'RE IN THIS MESS!

BUT THAT ONE RISKED *HIS* LIFE TO SAVE *MINE!*

AS YOU GO THROUGH LIFE, YOU MAKE RULES FOR YOURSELF--LIKE NOT ALIGNING YOURSELF WITH LOSERS--

PLEASE, MACHIKO...

--AND SOMETIMES THE RULES GO OUT THE WINDOW.

chapter

7

"I'll Remember You"

SOMETIMES WE CHOOSE WISELY, AND THE RESULTS PLEASE US.

OTHER TIMES OUR CHOICES GET US INTO *TROUBLE.*

THERE ARE TIMES WHEN WE'RE FORCED TO MAKE SPLIT-SECOND DECISIONS.

129

I DON'T KNOW WHETHER THE DECISION TO RESCUE THE BROKEN-TUSKED WARRIOR WAS A GOOD CHOICE OR A BAD ONE.

I DO KNOW IT WAS A *CRAZY* ONE. IT WAS AN *IMPOSSIBLE* RESCUE--EVEN A *TRAINED* PILOT WOULD HAVE BALKED.

BUT THE WARRIOR HAD PROVED HIMSELF *DIFFERENT* FROM THOSE OF HIS KIND WHO HAD KILLED HIROKI AND THE OTHERS, BY SAVING MIRIAM'S LIFE...

...AND, LIKE HIROKI, HE REFUSED TO GIVE UP FIGHTING.

I COULD *RESPECT* THAT.

WHUP WHUP WHUP

GRAB ON!

THIS IS *RIDICULOUS*, MIRIAM! I CAN'T HOLD US HERE MUCH LONGER--

--AND HE DOESN'T UNDER-STAND A *WORD* YOU'RE--

GRAB THE STRUT! WE'LL TAKE YOU TO SAFETY!

NEVER MIND! *HANG ON!*

OH, SHIT.

I REACTED INSTINCTIVELY, JERKING THE CONTROLS, AND THE COPTER SPUN ON ITS AXIS--JUST LIKE A HOVER BIKE.

BUT THAT'S WHERE THE SIMILARITIES ENDED.

WHUP WHUP

WKRUNCH!

I SHOULD HAVE GUESSED IT'D BE *YOU.* YOU'RE LUCKY TO BE *ALIVE,* LADY!

JESUS, WHO THE HELL TAUGHT YOU TO *FLY?*

NO ONE... YET.

WHERE'S MIRIAM?

LET'S GET *OUT* OF HERE! WE'RE GONNA BE UP TO OUR EYE-BALLS IN *BUGS* IN A MINUTE!

WHERE'S MIRIAM?

WHO?

Dr. REVNA-- THE WOMAN WHO WAS IN THE COPTER WITH ME! I'M NOT LEAVING WITHOUT HER!

I DIDN'T SEE ANYONE ELSE--

Oh, JESUS...

SOMEONE ELSE WAS DEAD...SOMEONE I'D CARED ABOUT...

...SOMEONE WHO'D DEPENDED ON ME.

Oh, MIRIAM...I'M SORRY...

GRAB THE STRUT--WE'LL PULL YOU TO SAFETY.

CONOVER AND STRANDBERG WERE THE LAST TWO PEOPLE IN PROSPERITY WELLS I'D HAVE WISHED TO BE STRANDED WITH, BUT NOW THAT MIRIAM WAS DEAD, THEY **WERE** THE LAST TWO PEOPLE.

SOMEHOW, THEY'D MISSED THE EVENTS OF THE PAST TWENTY-EIGHT HOURS. I BROUGHT THEM UP TO DATE...

I TOLD THEM WHAT I KNEW OF OUR COMPANION AND HIS KIND-- HOW THEY HAD ARRIVED EQUIPPED FOR A SAFARI. I EXPLAINED MY THEORY ABOUT THE **BUGS**-- AS THEY CALLED THEM-- AND THE WARRIORS BEING SOMEHOW **CONNECTED**.

ARE YOU SAYING **THEY** LET THOSE BUGS LOOSE ON A POPULATED PLANET SO THEY COULD **HUNT** THEM?

I DON'T BELIEVE HIS KIND **KNEW** THERE WERE HUMANS ON RYUSHI. WE HAVEN'T BEEN HERE LONG-- I **DOUBT** WE WERE HERE THE **LAST** TIME THEY DROPPED IN.

IN FACT, **OUR** PRESENCE PROBABLY SCREWED UP THEIR PLANS.

Oh, GREAT! I FEEL **SO** MUCH BETTER KNOWING THAT THIS WHOLE MESS WAS AN **ACCIDENT!**

HEY, AT LEAST HE'S ON **OUR** SIDE.

YEAH? PROBABLY ONLY UNTIL HE GETS **HUNGRY**...

I HALF EXPECTED A REPLAY OF THE LOST BATTLES I'D SEEN EARLIER...

...BUT THE BROKEN-TUSKED WARRIOR WAS NO INEXPERIENCED NOVICE.

HE MEASURED EVERY STEP--

--TIMED EVERY STRIKE.

THE OUTCOME OF THE BATTLE WAS NEVER IN DOUBT...

BLAM BLAM

BLAM BLAM

...I JUST DIDN'T HAVE TIME TO WAIT FOR IT.

SORRY--

CHIK

--BUT WE'VE GOT TO GO.

CHUK

HURRY!

EAST

OKAY, WE'RE IN. WHAT THE PLAN

WELL, THE COLONISTS MADE IT OUT SAFELY-- THAT'S THE MAIN THING. WE'VE GOT POWER HERE, WATER, AND FOOD.

I GUESS *WE'LL* JUST SEAL OUR- SELVES IN AND WAIT FOR THE MARINES.

WRONG. THE MARINES AREN'T COMING. SEEMS YOUR BOSS WANTS THE BUGS *ALIVE*--

LET ME *SEE* THAT!

OM: TAKASHI CHIGUSA NEW OSAKA

TO: MACHIKO NOGUC PROSPERITY WELLS

MOST IMMEDIATE. REQUEST FOR MARINE INTERVENTION DENIED. TAKE STEPS TO PRESERVE ALL SPECIMENS OF SPECIES DESCRIBED IN REVNA'S REPORT. PROCEED WITH MEASURES TO INSURE SAFETY OF ALL PERSONNEL, BUT TAKE NO ACTION AGAINST LIVI XT SPECIMENS. AWAIT INSTRUCTIONS FR HIGERU CHIGUSA, ARRIVI N MASUKO MARU.

SCREW *THAT* SHIT! I SAY WE SCRAM OUT OF HERE AND *JOIN* THE COLONISTS!

YEAH? AND HOW LONG BEFORE THE BUGS SPREAD INTO THE DESERT?

LOOK, I DON'T KNOW ABOUT YOU TWO, BUT I'M *TIRED* OF BEING *PUSHED AROUND.*

I WANT TO START PUSHING *BACK.*

SURE--WHAT'RE YOU GONNA DO? BURN DOWN THE WHOLE COMPLEX?

I DON'T THINK THAT'D WORK, SCOTT. TOO MANY OF THEM WOULD GET AWAY. IT'S GOT TO BE {coff} SOMETHING *FAST*...

MAYBE OUR *FRIEND* HERE HAS SOME IDEAS-- A DEATH RAY OR SOMETHING!

YOU TALKING ABOUT WHAT I *THINK* YOU ARE? *FORGET IT!*

DON'T HOLD OUT ON ME, CONOVER IF YOU KNOW A WAY TO STOP THOSE THINGS, YOU'D BETTER *TELL* ME!

I'M SERIOUS. I THINK MACHIKO {coff} HAD THE RIGHT IDEA WITH THE STAMPEDE-- THEY'RE *BUGS*, WHY NOT *CRUSH* 'EM?

HER FOOT WAS JUST {coff} TOO SMALL. YOU NEED SOMETHING {coff} *BIG ENOUGH* TO TAKE OUT THE WHOLE COMPLEX--*AND* THE LECTOR--AT ONCE.

COFF COFF

YOU KNOW HOW MANY *SHARES* I HAVE RIDING ON--

--TOM! WHA--?

NNNNG!

AAAAAAGGHHH

SKREE

SWIK

140

OH, GOD... TOM. JESUS...

LOOK...uh, I KNOW STRANDBERG WAS YOUR FRIEND, BUT YOU CAN'T GO TO PIECES YET. I NEED YOU FUNCTIONING.

BEFORE STRANDBERG... uh, HE WAS ABOUT TO TELL ME SOMETHING--SOMETHING THAT COULD WIPE OUT THE BUGS...

YOU DON'T GET IT, DO YOU? WHAT HAPPENED TO TOM... THAT THING THAT WAS INSIDE HIM...

WE WERE TOGETHER ON THE LECTOR. THAT MEANS I'VE GOT ONE INSIDE ME, TOO.

MY LIFE'S OVER. LEAVE ME ALONE.

YOU'RE NOT DEAD YET, CONOVER--AND WE STILL NEED YOUR HELP. WE'RE ALL IN THIS TOGETHER.

AND IF I DON'T HELP YOU? THINK YOU CAN THREATEN ME NOW?

NO, BUT MAYBE I CAN HELP YOU.

HELP ME? HOW? YOU A DOCTOR? YOU GONNA PERFORM SURGERY AND MAKE ME ALL BETTER?

NO... I CAN'T DO THAT. BUT YOU CAN HAVE A SHOT AT REVENGE--

--AND WHEN THE END COMES, I CAN MAKE IT QUICKER-- EASIER--FOR YOU.

"Okay, EVERYTHING YOU'LL NEED IS ON THE DISK."

"THANKS, CONOVER."

"GONNA BE TOUGH GETTING IN."

"DON'T WORRY, WE'LL FIND A WAY."

"I DON'T ⸰coff⸰ DOUBT THAT FOR A MINUTE, YOU KNOW, IF THIS WORKS, THE COMPANY'S GONNA BE PISSED."

"SCREW THE COMPANY."

"I WAS ⸰coff⸰ HOPING YOU'D SAY THAT."

WHUD

EAS

WHUD WHUMP

WHAM

HERE'S A ⸰coff⸰ A GOING-AWAY PRESENT-- A MAP OF THE LECTOR.

SOUNDS LIKE EVERY ⸰coff⸰ BUG IN THE PLACE IS TRYING TO GET IN.

IT'S ALL RIGHT-- WE'RE READY TO GO--

-- ALMOST...

⸰Coff⸰ I GUESS ⸰coff-coff⸰ IT'S TIME TO KEEP YOUR HALF OF THE BARGAIN... IF YOU CAN.

I CAN MAKE IT QUICKER-- EASIER-- FOR YOU.

NO. I MADE THE PROMISE. I'LL DO IT.

JESUS, IT'S WEIRD HEARING YOUR VOICE COME OUT OF HIM... ⸰coff⸰ JUST THOUGHT OF SOMETHING...⸰coff⸰ ...WHAT IF HE'S REALLY A SH--⸰coff-coff⸰

Aw, NEVER MIND. ⸰Coff⸰ Uhnn...!

JUST-- uhn!-- DO IT!

CONOVER--

--I'LL REMEMBER YOU.

IF MACHIKO WERE COMING, SHE'D BE HERE BY *NOW.*

MAYBE SOMEONE SHOULD GO BACK AND--

FORGET IT. THERE'S *NOTHING* WE CAN DO UNTIL THE MARINES SHOW UP.

IT COULD TAKE *WEEKS* FOR AN ASSAULT PARTY TO ARRIVE, ACKLAND.

FLYIN A RANGERS

IN THE MEANTIME, MACHIKO COULD BE *HURT*-- OR IN NEED OF *HELP.*

THOSE ARE THE CHANCES SHE TOOK WHEN SHE ACCEPTED THE JOB. CHI-GUSA CORP. IS RESPONSI-BLE FOR THE SAFETY OF THE *COLONISTS*-- NOT THE OTHER WAY AROUND.

YOU *BASTARD!* YOU CAN'T SHOVE THIS ALL OFF ON THE COMPANY--*YOU* HAD HE LIE TO DOC REVNA BOUT WHERE WE FOUND HOSE CREATURES! AND IT AS *YOUR* IDEA TO NEAK THOSE SICK HYNTH PAST QUAR-NTINE!

UH, LOOK, YOU KNOW WHAT A HARD-ASS NOGUCHI IS--

--I WAS JUST TRYING TO PROTECT MY INVESTMENT...uh...*OUR* INVESTMENTS...

SCREW OUR *INVEST-MENTS*-- I'VE GOT A *FAMILY!*

SAME HERE.

YOU CAN SAY WHAT YOU WANT ABOUT NOGUCHI, ACKLAND, BUT WHEN IT *CAME* DOWN TO IT, SHE RISKED HER LIFE TO SAVE ALL OF US-- INCLUDING *YOU!*

YOU'D BETTER PRAY SHE'S STILL *ALIVE* WHEN THIS IS ALL OVER.

SKREENK!

THE REVNAS' DEDICATION TO THEIR FRIENDS AND PATIENTS HAD COST THEM BOTH THEIR LIVES...

HIROKI HAD DIED FIGHTING FOR THE SAFETY OF THE COLONISTS...

COLLINS... MASON... RILEY... JOHNSON... AND ALL OF THE OTHERS HAD GIVEN THEIR LIVES FOR THE CONTINUED EXISTENCE OF PROSPERITY WELLS.

FROM THE TOP OF THE TOWER I LOOKED DOWN ON THE DE-SERTED SETTLEMENT. CAUGHT IN THE FIRST ROSY GLIMMERINGS OF DAWN, PROSPERITY WELLS LOOKED AS IT NEVER HAD, BE-NEATH THE HARSH GLARE OF RYUSHI'S DOUBLE SUNS --

--TRANQUIL AND COOL... LIKE A DREAM... OR A MEMORY.

IT WAS HARD TO BELIEVE THAT IN ANOTHER HOUR IT WOULD ALL BE GONE.

...AND THAT WE MIGHT BE *DEAD*.

NEVER MIND *THEM* -- GET TO THE *TRACTOR!*

OUR JOB WOULD HAVE BEEN A SIMPLE ONE IF THE COMMUNICATIONS SYSTEM IN THE OP CENTER HAD BEEN *OPERATIONAL*-- BUT MY COPTER RIDE HAD *TRASHED* THE MAIN ANTENNA.

STRANDBERG AND CONOVER'S PLAN REQUIRED AN *OFF-PLANET* TRANSMISSION --AND THAT MEANT A TRIP TO *THE LECTOR*--

KRASH

--BUG CENTRAL.

SKREEEEEE

SKKRUNCH

BIG SHIP...

FOR ALL HER SIZE, THE LECTOR WAS ONLY A *TUG*--

--*TINY* COMPARED TO THE MASSIVE REFRIGERATED *BARGE* SHE TOWED ACROSS THE HEAVENS.

SSSSS

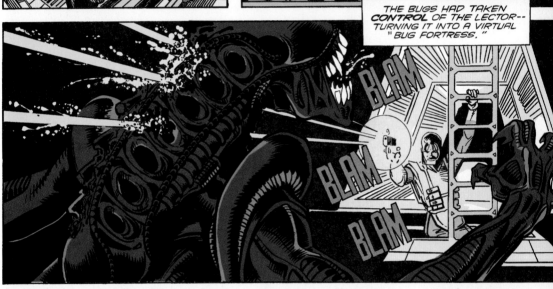

THE BUGS HAD TAKEN *CONTROL* OF THE LECTOR-- TURNING IT INTO A VIRTUAL "BUG FORTRESS."

BLAM
BLAM
BLAM
BLAM

BUT IF THE PLAN WORKED...

..., WE'D SHOW THE BUGS JUST HOW *SMALL* AND *EXPOSED* THEIR FORTRESS WAS.

KLIK

DO YOUR STUFF, COMPUTER.

WEAVER-- LOOK AT *THIS!* I'M PICKING UP A SIGNAL-- ORIGINATING FROM *PROSPERITY WELLS!*

A DISTRESS SIGNAL?

"NO... IT'S DIRECTED AT THE *LECTOR'S* ORBITAL BARGE... *NAVIGATIONAL INSTRUCTIONS!*"

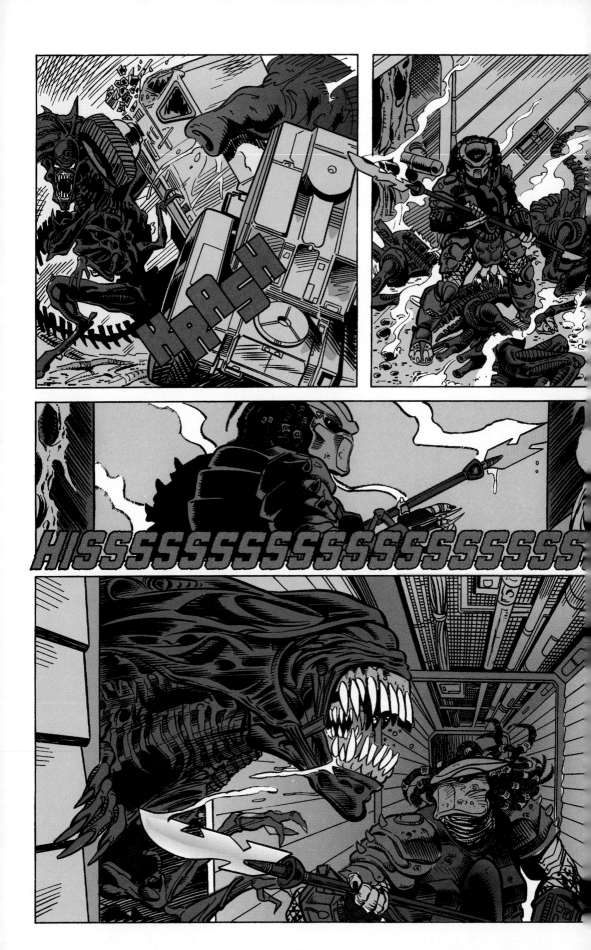

SHREEEEEEEE

--GIVE IT A *REST!*

BLAM BLAM

BLAM

BLAM

CAN'T LEAVE YOU ALONE FOR A MINUTE, CAN I?

FSSSTT FSSSS

TAKE IT EASY. FIVE SECONDS AND WE'RE GONE.

153

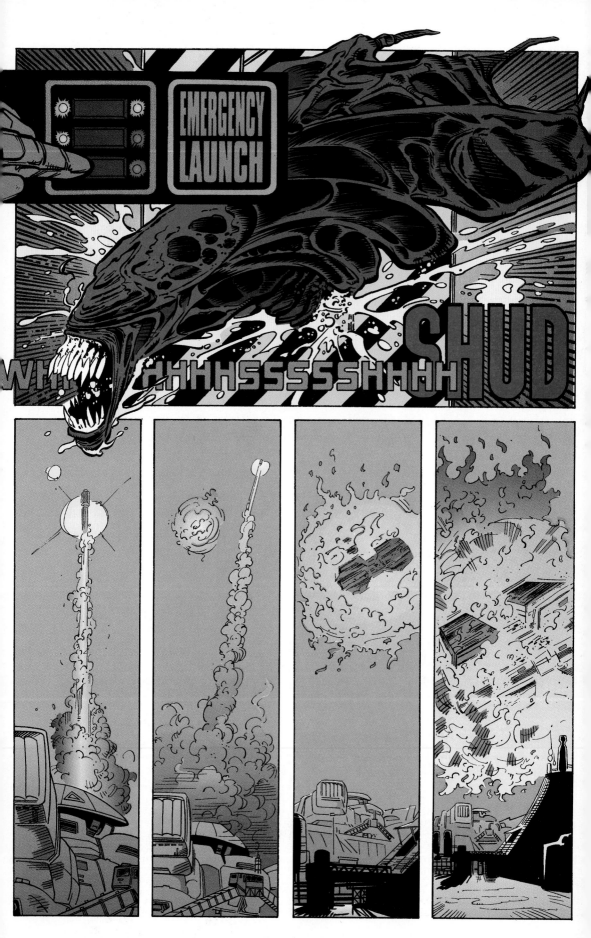

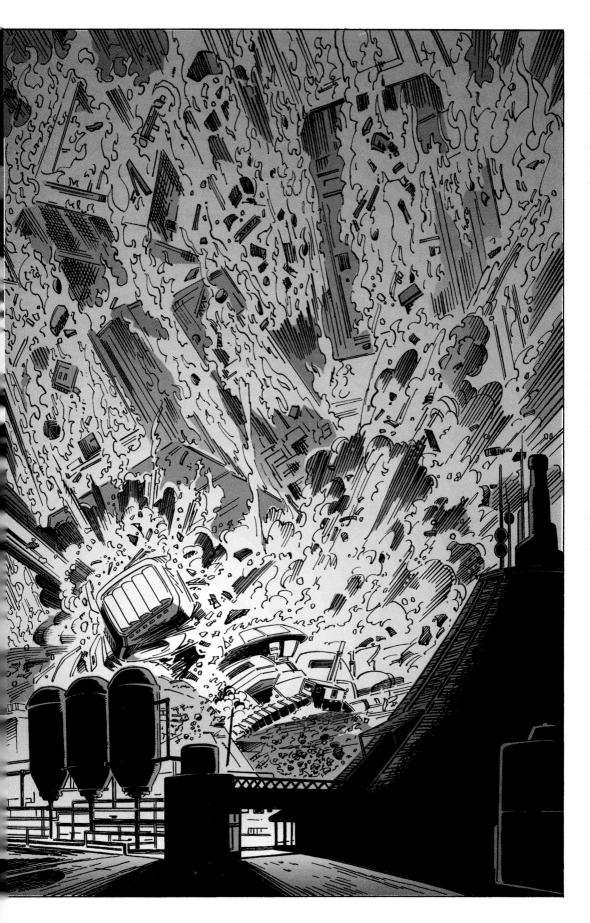

CRIK

SNAKT

...A GOING-AWAY PRESENT...

FSSSSHT

≥HUK≤... REMEMBER YOU...

AFTER THAT, THE COMPANY DECLARED PROSPERITY WELLS A "WRITE-OFF." THE COLONISTS WERE GIVEN PASSAGE TO A FRIENDLIER LOCATION IN THE RIGEL SYSTEM, AND CHIGUSA CORP. PULLED OUT OF CYGNI.

THEY SAID IT WAS UNDERSTOOD THAT MY ACTIONS WERE DICTATED BY NECESSITY-- BUT MY CONTRACT WAS BOUGHT OUT. I EXPECTED NO LESS.

THEY WERE NICE ENOUGH, THOUGH-- I WAS OFFERED PASSAGE BACK TO EARTH, AND WITH THE CREDITS FROM THE BUY-OUT, I COULD HAVE STARTED AGAIN.

I GUESS I SHOCKED THEM WHEN I SAID I WAS STAYING. IT JUST SEEMED THAT EVERYTHING I'D EVER CARED ABOUT-- OR LEARNED TO CARE ABOUT--WAS ON RYUSHI.

THAT WAS TWO YEARS AGO. "QUIET" DOESN'T BEGIN TO DESCRIBE THE EXPERIENCE OF HAVING AN ENTIRE PLANET TO ONESELF. BUT I'VE GOTTEN USED TO IT.

BESIDES, I KNOW THAT BROKEN TUSK'S PEOPLE WILL BE BACK SOMEDAY WITH A NEW BATCH OF BUGS.

THEN MAYBE I'LL DO A LITTLE HUNTING.

chapter

8

"Trophies"

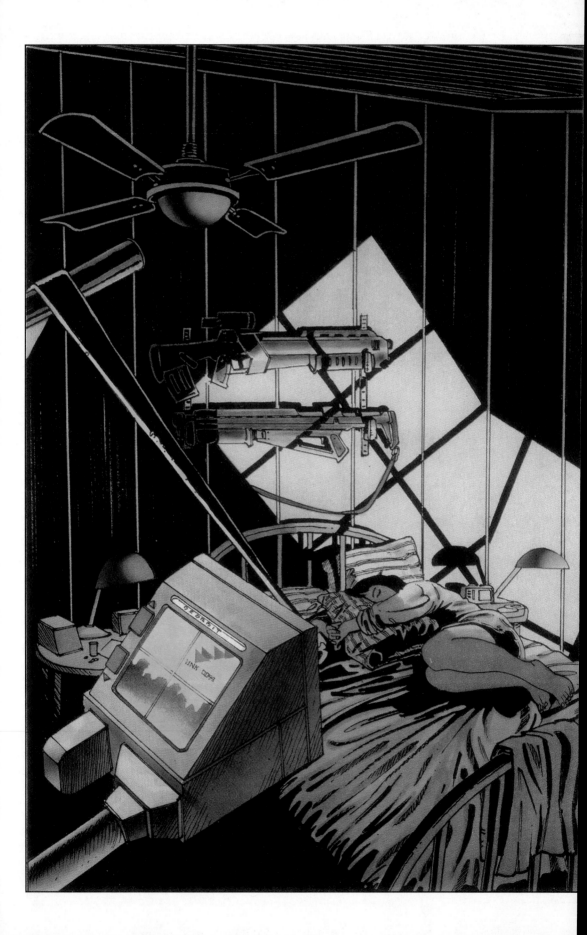

RRRRRRRRRRRRRRRRRRRRR

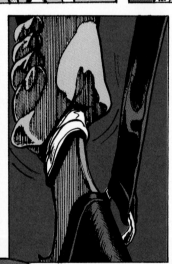

THEY'VE RETURNED.

FULLY AUTOMATED, VERY SLICK--LIKE STOCKING A POND WITH TROUT. I WONDER HOW LONG THIS HAS GONE ON--

--HOW MANY TIMES THIS SCENE HAS BEEN REPLAYED...

WHUMPF

SELF-DESTRUCTING. THAT EXPLAINS WHY CHIGUSA'S CLEAN-UP SQUAD COULDN'T FIND ANY TRACE OF A LANDER FOR THE BUGS.

IT SHOULDN'T BE LONG, NOW.

GO HOME, MILO! YOU DON'T WANT TO BE AROUND FOR THE NEXT PART.

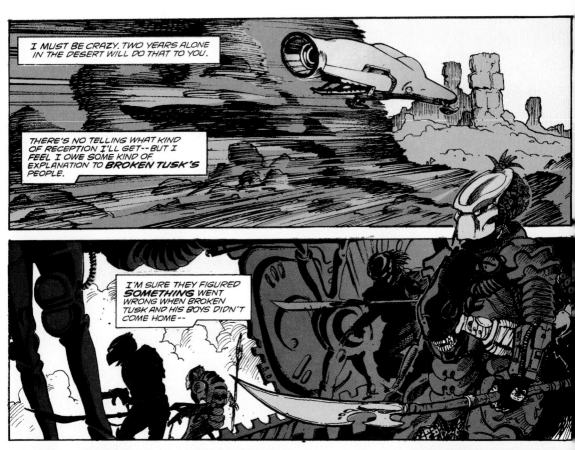

I MUST BE CRAZY. TWO YEARS ALONE IN THE DESERT WILL DO THAT TO YOU.

THERE'S NO TELLING WHAT KIND OF RECEPTION I'LL GET--BUT I FEEL I OWE SOME KIND OF EXPLANATION TO **BROKEN TUSK'S** PEOPLE.

I'M SURE THEY FIGURED **SOMETHING** WENT WRONG WHEN BROKEN TUSK AND HIS BOYS DIDN'T COME HOME--

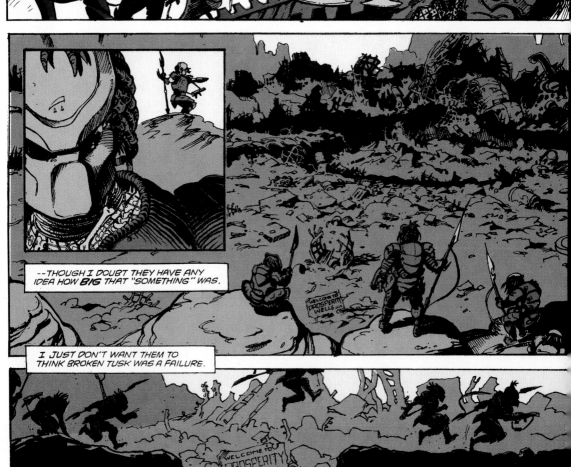

--THOUGH I DOUBT THEY HAVE ANY IDEA HOW **BIG** THAT "SOMETHING" WAS.

I JUST DON'T WANT THEM TO THINK BROKEN TUSK WAS A FAILURE.

HI, MIND
IF I TAG
ALONG?

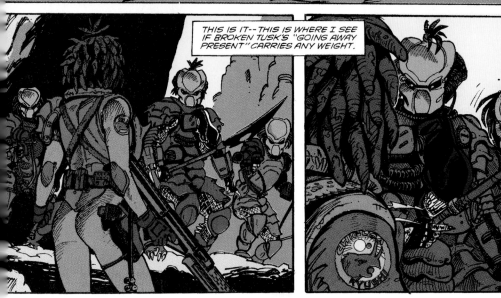

THIS IS IT--THIS IS WHERE I SEE
IF BROKEN TUSK'S "GOING AWAY
PRESENT" CARRIES ANY WEIGHT.

WAK

IF I DON'T END UP A *TROPHY* ON SOMEBODY'S WALL--

MAYBE I'LL GET THE CHANCE TO PICK UP A FEW TROPHIES OF MY *OWN*.

CONCEPTS
versus
REALITY

Behind the Scenes Tactics, Tension, and Trivia
by Randy Stradley

THREE LITTLE WORDS
Chris Warner said them first.

It was early 1989, and the Dark Horse crew was hashing over new projects and story lines in a company "bull session." Publisher Mike Richardson brought up a co-publishing venture proposed by another company. The teaming of the two suggested characters was something we couldn't quite visualize, but the proposal opened the door for a flood of "character versus character" suggestions—some less serious than others. We had gotten down to something like "Roachmill versus the Flaming Carrot," when Chris Warner said, "Aliens versus Predator." Something resembling a stunned silence followed. The pairing was such a natural one, it was a wonder it hadn't been the first idea to occur to us. Dark Horse was already publishing comics based on the films *Aliens* and *Predator,* both licensed from Twentieth Century Fox. Why not combine the two properties?

Within minutes Mike was on the phone to Pam North at Fox's licensing department for what he anticipated would be a long negotiating session. Pam's response, however, was immediate. "Aliens versus Predator? You mean like King Kong Versus Godzilla? Great, let's rock 'n' roll!" (Almost a year later, Capital City Distributors noted the team-up under "Deal of the Year" in their annual industry awards, saying, "Putting together the licensing deal for this

Above: One of Phill Norwood's early designs for new Predator armor that would protect the wearer from being spattered by the Aliens' acid blood.

combination was no small feat," an assumption we somehow neglected to contradict.)

PUTTING IT IN WRITING

A deal for a "guaranteed seller" such as *Aliens Vs. Predator* could have been seen merely as a license to print money (and, in fact, the series was successful beyond our wildest expectations), but Dark Horse has always believed that an interesting story is the only possible starting point for any project; we knew there would have to be more to the story than just Aliens and Predators beating the crap out of each other. To make the series entertaining as well as successful, there would have to be some kind of emotional hook — a character, or characters, that readers could identify with. For obvious reasons, a lead Alien character was out, and it was felt that making the lead character a Predator would not only be difficult, but would too greatly demystify the Predators. That left finding a way to introduce humans into the mix. Adding to whatever logistical problems already existed was the fact that in order to premiere the series in our anthology title Dark Horse Presents, Fox wanted an "Aliens-only" story and a "Predator-only" story to precede the first "Versus" story. Chris Warner and I, happily, were given the job of figuring out how to accomplish this—a pursuit made easier by the many intelligent suggestions supplied by Mike Richardson and Jerry Prosser.

Above: the original design for Ackland's truck. Don't expect anything like this out of detroit anytime soon.

One of the first concepts Chris Warner and I came up with was that of the Predators seeding life-bearing worlds with Alien eggs (with those eggs holding larval Queens carefully screened out of the mix). A limited number of eggs would make for an exciting, but controlled hunt — a rite of passage for young Predators. Slip an Alien Queen into the equation, and you had the makings for an even more exciting *un*controlled hunt.

TURNING IT INTO PICTURES

As work progressed, however, it became apparent that Chris' commitment to our then-new *Terminator* series was going to interfere with *Aliens Vs. Predator*. The deal with Fox for the team-up had a finite life span, and the final issue had to be on the stands before the contract expired. Chris,

Below: an early view of Prosperity Wells and *The Lector*.

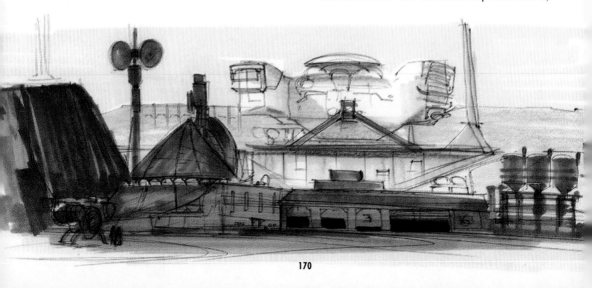

Two of Norwood's character designs. Above: Machiko, dressed for the Ryushi's weather. Below: Ackland. This drawing tells you everything you need to know about the rancher's personality.

reluctantly, bowed out of the project.

This put me in an uneasy position. I knew from editing Chris' work in the past that he took nothing for granted. No lapse in logic, no out-of-character action escaped his scrutiny. With Chris on the book, I knew that no matter what I eventually wrote, I'd come out looking good. Without him, I was unsure what would happen.

Enter Phill Norwood. Prior to *Aliens Vs. Predator*, Phill's only excursion into comics had been a 15-page collaboration with screenwriter Eric Luke ("Project: Overkill," *DHP* #30). Fortunately, Phill, whose primary occupation is creating storyboards and designs for films such as *Indiana Jones and the Temple of Doom, Back to the Future*, and *The Abyss*, was anxious to do more in comics.

At the '89 San Diego Comic Convention, Phill and I saw work by inker Karl Story. We tracked him to his table in "Artists' Alley," and asked him to join the project. I had already decided that I wanted Pat Brosseau to letter the series; I was impressed with his consistency, and he'd done good work on a number of other stories with little or no advance warning.

Midway through work on the first issue of the series, editor Diana Schutz came to work for Dark Horse — sparing me the dangerous job of editing any more of my own work.

But it wasn't all smooth sailing. After issue #2 of the series, newcomer Robert Campanella was brought in to ink the book and help get things back on a timely schedule, and by the end of issue #3, Terminator was once again interfering with *Aliens Vs. Predator*. This time it was Phill's involvement with *Terminator 2: Judgment Day*. Writer/director Jim Cameron wanted Phill to storyboard the film, and with a growing family to support, Phill was in no position to turn Cameron down. However, by this time, Chris Warner had completed his involvement with Dark Horse's *Terminator* mini-series and was able to step in and pencil the final issue — allowing Chris and I, after many years of friendship, to actually work together on a project for the first time.

The final member of the initial team was colorist Monika Livingston, whose work, unfortunately, is not evident in this volume. (Everyone involved was generally unhappy with the "fit" of the blue-lined color in the separations in the series. During the planning of this volume, it was discovered that advances in computer technology would make it nearly as cost-efficient to recolor the entire story as to have new laser-scan separations made from the existing colors. There were also nearly forty pages of material that had never been colored: the three "prequel" stories from *DHP* #34-36, and the epilogue that was published as part of the *DHP Fifth Anniversary Special*. The team at In-Color, working from color suggestions by Phill Norwood, have done an amazing job of coloring this collection with their state-of-the-art computer system.)

DETAILS

Distinguishing between a writer and an artist's contributions to a story isn't always easy. Some things, of course, are obvious: the writer decides what happens and what the characters say while it's happening. Writers, if they are doing their job, also determine pacing, mood, and point of view. It's from this point that the artist takes over, but Phill's contributions to the story itself —

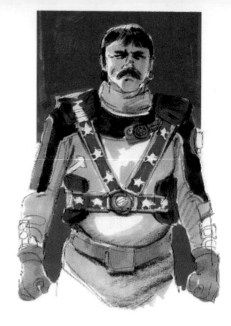

above and beyond the visual realization of it — cannot be understated. The Doctors Revna were his idea. So was the stampede. Ditto having the Predators' armor and weapons fashioned from segments of Alien exoskeleton (making them resistant to the Aliens' acid blood), the welcome party for the crew of the spaceship/slaughterhouse *The Lector* (which, by the way, I so-named because of that word's onomatopoeic resemblance to Lecter — as in Hannibal Lecter — Thomas Harris' compelling character from his novels "Red Dragon" and "Silence of the Lambs"), and dozens of other ideas that, however seemingly small, fleshed

Above right, and below: more of Phill's character and costume designs. Some of the suits were intended to recycle water from perspiration.

out the story and provided me with hooks to hang the action on. (It was also Phill's idea to base the appearance of the character Scott Conover, one of the Lector's pilots, on director Jim Cameron, whom Phill had worked for on *The Abyss.* Ironically, by the time Phill's pencils were inked, the Conover character also bore a passing resemblance to the friend I had named him after.)

Of course, the greatest advantage in collaborating with Phill is his ability to create something believable from my meager instructions. For example, it was very easy for a me, as a writer, to say, "Machiko and Hiroki ride off on hover bikes" — after all, flying contraptions of one sort or another have been standard-issue equipment in comics for years. But the hover bikes that Phill came up with actually look as though they could work; they have weight and bulk, room for an engine and fuel supply, and rotors large enough to lift something their size off the ground. Phill's attention to detail and design imbued every aspect of the Prosperity Wells setting with an air of believability that virtually assured suspension of disbelief on the part of the reader.

As you can see by the illustrations accompanying this article (taken from Phill's initial sketches and designs), a great deal of thought went into the creation of characters, costuming, and technology to make everything in the story consistent with both the *Alien/Aliens* "universe" and the *Predator* "universe."

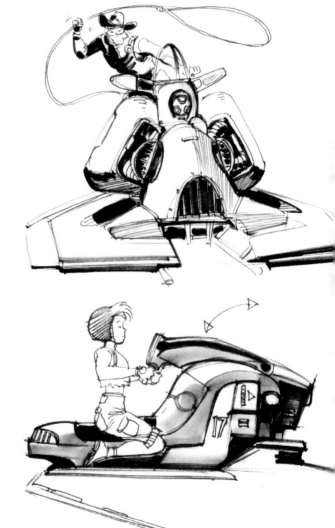

This page and over leaf: more of Phill's studies for the hover bikes used throughout the story. The illustration at the top of this page was only Phill's second second sketch for a flying vehicle. Note that all are designed so that they can be ridden standing, sitting, or kneeling.

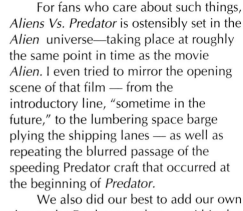

For fans who care about such things, *Aliens Vs. Predator* is ostensibly set in the *Alien* universe—taking place at roughly the same point in time as the movie *Alien*. I even tried to mirror the opening scene of that film — from the introductory line, "sometime in the future," to the lumbering space barge plying the shipping lanes — as well as repeating the blurred passage of the speeding Predator craft that occurred at the beginning of *Predator*.

We also did our best to add our own touches to the Predator mythos — within the parameters we'd already established for ourselves: avoid laying down any hard and fast cultural guidelines that would lock the Predators into prosaic actions in future stories or, worse yet, would be contradicted by the second Predator film that we knew was in the works. Sending the young Predators on a ritual hunt (complete with a "blooding" with acid blood!) fit these criteria, and led logically to the introduction of Broken Tusk (someone had to lead the hunt), as well as allowing for conflict between Broken Tusk and his charges when, bereft of his leadership, they break Predator hunting code and go on a killing spree among the human population of Ryushi (a name which is a bastardization of the Japanese word for "hunter").

Working backwards from those concepts led us to the idea of Broken Tusk and the other mature Predators battling among themselves for rights to particular hunting grounds (planets that had perhaps been used again and again for the ritual Alien hunts), an event that worked well to fulfill Fox's desire for a Predator-only story.

One surprising aspect of both the *Alien* and *Predator* movie series is that while they appear on the surface to be nothing more than action-adventure films, both series are rich in subtle clues to a larger world beyond that with which the stories are concerned. It seemed each time I needed a piece of equipment or a motive to move the story ahead, I realized that what I needed already existed in the films. And as they made their mark on this story, it appears *Aliens Vs. Predator* made its mark in motion pictures, as well (remember the Predator's trophy case in *Predator 2*?).

SOMETIME IN THE FUTURE...

At the outset, I believed the Aliens-Predator pairing would be good for one story only—a novelty. By the end of the series, I had come up with a number of ways that entertaining stories could be made to revolve around the idea of these two alien races in conflict with one another. Apparently I wasn't the only one. Currently, writer Chris Claremont is writing an *AVP* maxi-series; Mike Richardson is working on a four-issue comics story that's also raising eyebrows in Hollywood; Dave Gibbons and Mike Mignola are teaming to produce a one-shot story; and, in our second outing together, Chris Warner and I are working on the direct sequel to the story you've just read, which is presently being serialized in the pages of the *Dark Horse Insider*. It appears that the volume you hold in your hands tells of but one battle in a prolonged war. ◆

MACHIKO AND FRIEND